MINERALS

WHAT YOUR BODY REALLY NEEDS & WHY

GEORGE L. REDMON, PhD, ND

AVERY PUBLISHING GROUP

Garden City Park • New York

The information, advice, and procedures contained in this book are based upon the research and the personal and professional experiences of the authors. They are not intended as a substitute for consulting with your physician or other health-care provider. The publisher and author are not responsible for any adverse effects or consequences resulting from the use of any of the suggestions, preparations, or procedures discussed in this book. All matters pertaining to your physical health should be supervised by a health care professional. It is a sign of wisdom, not cowardice, to seek a second or third opinion.

Cover designer: Doug Brooks
In-house editor: Dara Stewart
Typesetter: Gary A. Rosenberg
Printer: Paragon Press, Honesdale, PA

Avery Publishing Group
120 Old Broadway
Garden City Park, NY 11040
1-800-548-5757
www.averypublishing.com

Library of Congress Cataloging-in-Publication Data

Redmon, George L., 1952–
    Minerals: what your body really needs and why / George Redmon.
        p.   cm.
    Includes bibliographical references and index.
    ISBN 0-89529-863-5
    1. Minerals in the body.   2. Minerals in human nutrition.   3. Mineral metabolism.   I. Title.

QP533.R43   1999
616.3'92—dc21   99-18141
                                                                                    CIP

Copyright © 1999 by George Redmon

Printed in the United States of America

10   9   8   7   6   5   4   3   2   1

CONTENTS

*This book is dedicated to Della,
whose physical struggle with pain, disease,
and a life of constant medical care inspired me
to search for the truth. Her courage and our
misunderstanding of the cause and origin of
disease finally made me realize that people's
greatest enemy is not the disease, it is
our inability to realize our individual
innate potential to prevent or slow
down its destructive forces.*

May she rest in peace.

ACKNOWLEDGMENTS

I am greatly indebted to Kevin and Jennifer Noel (Word Wizards, Ltd.) and their secretarial support staff for the exceptional editorial and copy work done on this manuscript.

I also wish to express my deep and lasting appreciation to Dr. Victoria Wilson, R.Ph., M.P.H., for her valuable assistance and guidance in the preparation of this book, and to Mr. Rudy Shur of Avery Publishing for his consideration in providing the platform for this book.

I am also indebted to countless researchers who have influenced me and have laid the foundation for "critical thinking" regarding the role of nutritional supplementation as a viable means to preventative health care. I am sincerely grateful to the following individuals who have supplied the emotional fuel, and in some cases, their expertise and knowledge, without which this project could not have been completed: Dr. Lloyd Clayton, N.D., founder and president of American Holistic College of Nutrition, Clayton School of Natural Healing, Birmingham, Alabama; Dr. Willard E. Downham, Jr., E.D., director of Adult School, Washington Township Public Schools, Sewell, New Jersey; Dean Eugene Jones, Division of Continuing Education, Burlington County College, Pemberton, New Jersey; Dr. Barry Persky, E.D., New York City University Department of Education, New York; Ms. Jessie F. Pervall, Thomas Jefferson Medical University, Department of Graduate Studies, Philadelphia, Pennsylvania; Dr. Pamela Peters, Ph.D., The Center for Stress, Pain, and Wellness Management, Wilmington, Delaware; and Dr. Marcia B. Steinhaur, Ph.D., Department of Health and Human Services, Walden University, Minneapolis, Minnesota.

PREFACE

My search to find the possible rejuvenating benefits that minerals may have provided started some twenty years ago. About a month following my college graduation, a lump appeared on the left side of my neck. This occurence changed my life dramatically. After careful examination by several medical specialists, tests revealed that I had Hodgkin's disease, a form of cancer that affects the lymph nodes.

The lymph nodes are small, roundish bodies in the lymphatic system that supply white blood cells to the blood and remove foreign matter from the lymph. The lympathic system can be thought of as a commander to the various troops, which are called into action once the body recognizes an antigen (a substance the body perceives as foreign) to fight off foreign invaders. Nature has strategically placed the lymph nodes near and around vital organs and in close proximity to sites of various metabolic reactions. As you have probably realized, once this command post is compromised and left untreated in a cancerous state, death will eventually occur, since the body will be unable to protect itself.

At the conclusion of my treatment and subsequent recovery period, I found that my immune response was not quite as effective as it once was. Even as the months passed and I regained much of my strength, hair, and skin tone, I became suspectible to seemingly every-thing—recurring colds, fatigue, allergic reactions, loss of taste sensations and overall appetite, and bouts of mild depression. When I discussed these concerns with my personal physician, he suggested that I stay on a bal-anced diet, get plenty of rest, and consume plenty of flu-ids, especially water. He also suggested that when I real-ly began hitting empty, to go to his office for, as he called them, "booster shots" and maybe an "IV" (intravenous fluids) if necessary.

I initially had success with the plan but quickly became weary with the constant trips to his office. I began to think, "Why wait until my immune system begins to wear down and become sluggish? Why wait until my immune response's reaction time slows down? Why not start a daily rebuilding program? But more important, why did the doctor suggest I drink lots of flu-ids, what was in those booster shots, and why did I feel a lot better after the 'IV'"?

Finding the answers to these seemingly trivial ques-tions was the turning point in my investigations into nutritional therapy, immunity, and especially the elec-trolytic (electricity producing) action of water-soluble mineral elements and their health-restoring benefits. After incorporating mineral supplements into a sensible food program, my situation changed dramatically. There was a complete reversal and acceleration of my recovery.

Over the years, as I began to gain knowledge about the life-giving attributes of minerals, I have found that much of the current focus on nutritional supplementation places little emphasis on their use. Although new discoveries about nutritional supplements and the important role they play in preventive and restorative health care are mounting, there is one scientific fact about minerals that we tend to forget: They are responsible for creating and maintaining a healthy internal environment that enables other nutrients to flourish and do their jobs.

Without the health problems I encountered early in life, my thirst for knowledge about the beneficial attributes of minerals, especially in electrolyte form, may have never materialized. It is my hope that *Minerals: What Your Body Really Needs and Why* will spur new interest and continued research into the importance of these small but powerful substances.

Read on and find out why minerals are truly nature's biological keys to health!

INTRODUCTION

Most scientists assume that all life arose out of the sea, a solution rich in minerals that covers 70 percent of the earth. There are over 60 trillion cells in our bodies. Each one needs an array of mineral elements for its functioning and integrity. In fact, as cited by Gillian Martlew, N.D., the author of *Electrolytes: The Spark of Life*, 5 percent of each cell is composed of minerals. In essence, mineral elements are part of the machinery that propels and perpetuates the metabolic cycles (the sum of all processes in an organism by which energy is made available to sustain life processes) that keep us alive.

Thus, no life could develop if minerals were excluded. They provide structural and functional support for the cells. Nature furnishes optimum quantities of each mineral in the cells so that minimal amounts of energy are needed to keep the levels constant; however, factors such as poor soil quality and poor lifestyle habits make maintaining these blood mineral levels difficult. Any quantity less than the optimum would eventually lead to a deficiency state and to cellular malfunction.

As nutritional science developed, more minerals were seen as being essential to human life. Minerals needed in larger quantities, such as calcium, phosphorus, sodium, potassium, and magnesium, were recognized relatively early. They are termed *bulk, major,* or *macro minerals.* Other minerals, required in such minuscule amounts that it was impossible to measure them accurately by the primitive methods used at the time, were recognized later. They are called *trace elements, trace minerals,* or *micro minerals* and include iron, cobalt, iodine, molybdenum, copper, selenium, zinc, manganese, and chromium. Both bulk minerals and trace minerals are involved in nearly every physiological reaction. For example, they carry oxygen in the blood and help nails and hair grow. Or a mineral such as calcium gives structural rigidity to bones and teeth. Often, minerals are associated with the vitamins as coenzymes (helpers to the enzymes).

Minerals: What Your Body Really Needs and Why will show you how to protect yourself from illness by offsetting possible deficiencies of minerals. The book is divided into two parts. Part One discusses the vital role that minerals, especially in their electrolyte form, play in initiating, controlling, and sustaining many of life's processes. It explains the attributes of the many key minerals. It explains minerals' antioxidant effects—their abilities to neutralize the harmful effects of the highly reactive and damaging substances known as free radicals. Uncontrolled free-radical aggression is related to the onset and progression of over sixty age-related chronic degenerative diseases. Part Two takes a look at the individual minerals. It reveals the health-restorative abilities of the individual mineral elements and the possible medical applications of their use in combating a number of today's chronic health problems.

As stated, *Minerals: What Your Body Really Needs and Why* is designed to make you aware of the vital roles mineral electrolytes play in controlling countless bodily processes. To paraphrase mineral researcher Dr. George W. Crane, M.D.: It is entirely possible that water-soluble trace elements will be the greatest medical innovation in preventive and restorative health care in the twenty-first century.

Part One

The Nature of Minerals

Scientists have always known that we can live for an extended period of time without food, but not without water. This is because water contains minerals, a source of life-giving nourishment for the body.

Carbohydrates, proteins, lipids (fats, fatty acids, cholesterol), and vitamins are all *organic* (pertaining to or derived from living organisms) substances. Although the above organic nutrients play a major role in the preservation of health, a group of *inorganic* (nonliving) chemical elements are responsible for initiating the action of their organic counterparts. In essence, in the body, they act as control agents and contribute to energy production, body building, and maintenance. These inorganic catalysts are widely distributed in nature and are known as minerals.

These minerals play a significant role in the continuation of life processes. Without the proper minerals, our bodies could not function. Part One of this book will take a look at the value of minerals in our bodies. It will examine their functions, their importance in electrolyte form, their antioxidant capabilities, and factors that affect their absorption.

1 MINERALS– NATURE'S BIOLOGICAL CATALYSTS

Our physical well-being is more directly dependent upon minerals we take into our systems than upon calories or vitamins, or upon the precise proportion of starch, protein, or carbohydrates we consume.

—*U.S. Senate Document Number 264*
Published in 1936

Many of nature's minerals are necessary components of human nutrition that activate and control many physiological processes. In fact, according to Dr. Erwin DiCyan, Ph.D., author of *Vitamins in Your Life and the Micronutrients,* we cannot live without these inorganic substances. Additionally, investigations by nutritional experts have revealed that the body needs much larger quantities of many minerals than vitamins every day, a fact that still eludes many of us. I quote Dr. Michael Schwartz, of the Inner Health Group in San Antonio, Texas: "It amazes me how few people take minerals. Even more surprisingly is the number of 'health food' people who think they are getting enough minerals in their one-a-days. It is absolutely shocking when you realize how little people know about the importance of minerals in maintaining excellent health."

Just what are mineral elements? Where do they come from? Why are they important? What metabolic process are they involved with? Does the body manufacture them? In this chapter, I will answer these and other pertinent questions concerning the dynamic aspects of these powerful substances.

WHAT ARE MINERALS?

Minerals are inorganic (not produced by plants or animals) elements that are vital for human life. Elements are substances that cannot be broken down into simpler substances. They are the basic components of all larger compounds. Due to their varying degrees of need and content in the body, scientists refer to minerals as *macro* or *micro* minerals. Those minerals present in larger amounts are known as the major or macro minerals. These minerals are needed in the body in dosages exceeding 100 milligrams. Minerals needed in minute quantities (usually less than 100 milligrams) are referred to as the trace elements, trace minerals, micro minerals, or inorganic micronutrients. All of these names are interchangeable.

The essential major minerals are:

- Calcium.
- Chloride.
- Magnesium.
- Phosphorus.
- Potassium.
- Sodium.
- Sulfur.

The essential micro minerals are:

- Chromium.
- Cobalt.
- Copper.
- Fluorine.
- Iodine.

- Iron.
- Manganese.
- Molybdenum.
- Selenium.
- Zinc.

According to Dominick Bosco, author of *The People's Guide to Vitamins and Minerals*, scientists don't yet know all the minerals the body needs to maintain life. Dr. Joel Wallach, N.D., an established author, lecturer, and renowned nutritionist known as the "Mineral Doctor," adamantly argues that we need the sixty or so minerals known to humankind. Researchers thus far have not been able to determine in humans if all of these minerals are essential—at least not yet. "Essential" here refers to the fact that these minerals are vital for the proper functioning of the body and cannot be made or manufactured by the body, thus requiring that they be acquired through the diet. Current research, however, revealed seventeen minerals that are considered essential.

Nutritional experts use the following criteria to determine if a mineral should be considered essential.

- A dietary lack creates specific deficiency symptoms that respond when the mineral is reinstated.

- Its addition to a purified diet improves health.

- It plays a role as a necessary component of tissue, fluids, or regulatory processes.

- It is an essential part of some other essential nutrient.

These substances, which appear to be inert (not readily reactive with other elements) in comparison with organic vitamin compounds, are responsible for a vast array of metabolic functions in the body. Metabolism is concerned with the sum total of all anabolic (building up) and catabolic (breaking down) chemical reactions within the body.

MINERALS AND HEALTH

Minerals are components of body tissue and fluids that work in combination with enzymes, hormones, vitamins, and other vital transport substances. Some minerals are cofactors (helpers) for enzymes, which are catalysts for every reaction that occurs in the body. Many of these minerals participate in nerve transmission; muscle contraction; the maintenance of cell permeability, tissue rigidity and structure, and acid-base balance; blood formation; fluid regulation and movement across cell membranes; protein metabolism; and energy production.

Ionized sodium and potassium (atoms having a positive or negative electrical charge) maintain a balance of body fluids inside and outside the cells. Calcium and phosphorus provide structure for the framework of the body. Oxygen-hungry iron composes hemoglobin (protein that gives red blood cells their color). The mineral iodine is a constituent of thyroid hormone, which, in turn, controls the overall rate of metabolism.

Additionally, in 1957, researchers discovered in animals that the onset of diabetes could be prevented with two minerals—chromium and vanadium. Studies conducted by Dr. Gary Evans, a biochemist at Bemidji State University in Minnesota, have confirmed that chromium picolinate (a supplemental form of chromium) could be very useful in treating Type II diabetes. In this type of diabetes, naturally occurring insulin is not as effective at controlling blood sugar levels as it should be.

Furthermore, Dr. Sherry Rogers, M.D., asserts that studies show the cause of some people's hypertension (high blood pressure) is an undiagnosed magnesium deficiency. In addition, Dr. Anthony J. Cichoke, D.C., D.A.C.B.N., a respected authority on nutrition, maintains that the mineral zinc acts as a powerful antioxidant, fighting the harmful effects of free radicals. Free radicals are highly reactive molecules, formed as by-products during normal metabolism. Uncontrolled, these free radicals can cause numerous disorders, including Alzheimer's disease, arthritis, atherosclerosis (hardening of the arteries), heart disease, cancer, and accelerated aging.

Based on past and present data, researchers are just beginning to have a broader appreciation and understanding of the critical roles of these inorganic elements. By no means are these minerals static (not moving or changing in the body). They are major players in the maintenance of the body's internal equilibrium, known as homeostasis.

Many of us believe that we can sustain life's processes on one meal a day. Following such a nutritional plan will cause severe mineral deficiencies, leaving you susceptible to an array of deficiency diseases. To compound this problem, many medical experts still contend that eating three balanced meals will provide your body with all the nutrients it needs. While this is theoretically possible, studies have proven that this "mythical diet" in today's society is just that—a myth. In fact, a recent study at the University of California at Berkeley revealed that 70 percent of men and 80 percent of women eat foods that contain less than two-thirds of the Recommended Dietary Allowance (RDA) of one or more of the fifteen vitamins and minerals considered essential to health. The RDAs are nutritional standards established by the National Research Council of the U.S. Department of Health and Human Services to prevent deficiencies of essential nutrients.

MAINTAINING MINERAL BALANCE IN THE BODY

Investigations into the interactions of minerals within the human body have substantiated the effects of mineral imbalances. If there is too little or too much of one mineral, all other minerals are affected, starting a chain reaction of mineral imbalances and illnesses. In other words, when minerals are in balance and are in their proper ratios, they neutralize the potentially harmful effects of their counterparts—sort of a check and balance system.

According to Gillian Martlew, N.D., author of *Electrolytes: The Spark of Life*, delicate mineral balance is easily disrupted. In fact, research carried out on stress at a university in Bethesda, Michigan, and the United States Department of Agriculture (USDA) Human Research Center in Maryland produced clinical evidence that periods of physical and psychological stress deplete trace minerals. These studies also revealed that it can take up to seven days to return these imbalances to normal levels once stressful episodes had subsided. It is this disarrangement and interruption of these switches or keys that scientists believe cause some of the disease states to exist and flourish.

Many minerals have similar physical and chemical properties. As a result, when there is a deficiency of certain essential minerals or an overabundance of some of the more toxic minerals, the more toxic ones, like cadmium, silver, arsenic, and lithium, can actually take the place of some similar, more essential minerals. For example, cadmium may replace zinc, silver may replace copper, lithium may replace sodium, and arsenic may replace phosphorus. When zinc is not present or cadmium is more abundant, cadmium can inactivate zinc enzymes, which are involved in controlling numerous metabolic processes.

Because of the checks-and-balances system among the minerals, which helps prevent deficiencies and toxicities, no mineral should be taken alone. In order that we have optimal health, we must consider the absolute minimal requirements for each mineral, the amounts we actually take in, and levels that may be toxic when assessing our necessary mineral dosages.

One built-in mechanism the body has to offset possible mineral toxicity is hydrochloric acid (HCl). The body is capable of forming some agents to bind with a small amount of inorganic minerals to aid their absorption into the bloodstream and can do so only if it has sufficient hydrochloric acid (HCl). If this acid is lacking, these minerals cannot be used and may be stored in unwanted places, such as joints, causing arthritis.

There is mounting evidence that shows that this critical digestive aid's production diminishes as we age. Because of these findings, many health officials recommend that everyone age 40 and older supplement their diets with hydrochloric acid. HCl's interaction with minerals is crucial to maintaining the body's internal homeostatic levels of them. For example, hydrochloric acid liberates iron from food and converts it to the form required for absorption.

If you are deficient in hydrochloric acid, you may run the risk of improperly digested foods, as well as loss of the body's ability to extract the valuable minerals, vitamins, and proteins it needs. Some symptoms of low levels of hydrochloric acid in the gastrointestinal tract include frequent heartburn, reduced immunity, lack of energy, and frequent gas and bloating. Hydrochloric acid can be purchased at your local vitamin, drug, or health-food store as a food supplement called betaine hydrochloric acid. For those persons suffering from a stomach or digestive disorder, it may be wise to check with your health-care professional first before using this supplement.

Dr. Andrew Weil, M.D., considered to be one of the world's foremost experts on alternative medicine, mind-body interactions, and medical botany, states that it is important that you become conscious of the dynamics and internal change or disrupted equilibrium that occurs almost endlessly within. As expressed by Dr. Weil:

> *We are an island of change in a sea of change, subject to cycles of rest and activity, of secretions of hormones, and of the rise and fall of power drives, subjected to noise, irritants, agents of disease, electrical and magnetic fields, the deterioration of age, and emotions. The variables are infinite, and all is in flux and motion. That equilibrium occurs even for an instant in such a system is miraculous, since equilibrium is constantly destroyed and re-created.*

Dr. Weil went on to say that far from being simply the absence of disease, health is a dynamic and harmonious equilibrium of all the elements and forces making up and surrounding a human being. However, past and present data still reiterate the fact that mineral electrolytes are our bodies' first line of defense. They are the catalysts responsible for maintaining this complex balancing act.

DEFICIENT SOILS—DEFICIENT PEOPLE

As divulged by the United States Senate, and as quoted in the opening of this chapter, our mineral intake is more important than our intake of vitamins, calories, proteins, or carbohydrates. Duped into believing that our diets would suffice as a source of nutrients, many medical experts may have failed to mention to you that as a result of past and present farming methods, there are virtually no nutritional minerals in our farm and range soils. As a result, the crops that are grown there are mineral deficient, and the animals and people who eat these mineral-deficient crops get mineral-deficiency diseases. Many of today's long-term degenerative diseases, such as arthritis, heart disease, hypertension, and arteriosclerosis are caused by nutritional deficiencies.

What is most frightening is that the findings that our soils are mineral-deficient were made public some *sixty-one* years ago. These findings were not reported in some obscure medical journal or hidden deep within some historical archive. These findings were reported and made public by the United States Senate and can be found in U.S. Senate Document 264, published in 1936, as quoted below.

> *This talk about minerals is novel and quite startling. In fact, a realization of the importance of minerals in food is so new that the text books on nutritional dietetics contain very little about it. Nevertheless, it is something that concerns all of us, and the further we delve into it, the more startling it becomes.*
>
> *You'd think, wouldn't you, that a carrot is a carrot—that one is about as good as another as far as nourishment is concerned? But it isn't; one carrot may look and taste like another and yet be lacking in the*

particular mineral element which our system requires and which carrots are supposed to contain.

No longer does a balanced and fully nourishing diet consist merely of so many calories or certain vitamins or a fixed proportion of starches, proteins, and carbohydrates. We know that our diet must contain in addition something like a score of mineral salts.

It is bad news to learn from our leading authorities that 99% of the American people are deficient in these minerals, and that a marked deficiency in any one of the more important minerals acutally results in disease. Any upset of the balance, any considerable lack of one or another element, however microscopic the body requirement may be, and we sicken, suffer, shorten our lives.

To improve the quality and quantity of the minerals in our soils today, researchers are frantically trying to bring about changes. President Clinton signed into law The Food Quality Protection Act on August 3, 1996. On the surface, this appears to be an act that would ensure the quality and safety of our food. The key provision of this act, however, is the repeal of the zero-pesticide-tolerance Delaney Clause, which bars the use of any pesticide that may cause cancer in processed foods, no matter how little the risk posed by the pesticide's use is. Instead, this act allows the use of pesticides that pose less than a one-in-one-million risk of causing cancer over a lifetime of exposure in raw and unprocessed foods. The governing factor for acceptable allowable levels will now be the health risk that pesticide poses to children. In addition to their cancer-causing effects, pesticides also deplete nutrients, particularly minerals, from our soils, and thus, our food.

In addition, our farmland is fertilized with NPK

(nitrogen, phosphorus, and potassium). Again, on the surface, this may seem beneficial. However, there should be at least sixty minerals in soil, most of which are depleted due to modern farming methods. Then only three are replenished with the use of NPK. Farmers are paid for tons and bushels of crops; however, no cash incentives are paid to farmers to insure that there are sixty minerals in the soil.

Recent studies conducted at the Earth Summit in Rio (June 1992), which compared the mineral content of soils today with soils 100 years ago, revealed some startling facts. Researchers found that in African soils, there were 74-percent less minerals present in the soil today than there were 100 years ago. Asian soils have 76-percent less, European soils have 72-percent less, South American soils have 76-percent less, and the soils in the United States and Canada contain 85-percent less minerals today than they did 100 years ago. These statistics show that our soils are not the "nutrition fields of dreams" on which our ancestors flourished.

The evidence clearly shows that we as a nation, as well as our lands, are mineral deficient. Another excerpt from Senate Document Number 264 reads, "Laboratory test prove that the fruits, the vegetables, the grain, the eggs, and even the milk and meat of today are not what they were a few generations ago" (which doubtlessly explains why our forefathers thrived on a selection of foods that would starve us!).

CONCLUSION

Past and present research has confirmed that minerals are absolutely necessary to maintain health. They are involved with countless metabolic and enzymatic reactions, which either start, control, or help maintain important bodily functions. They are also involved with pro-viding the necessary materials that help to maintain and build strong bones, teeth, and tissue structures. Data have also established the need to constantly supply the body with these mineral elements through diet, due to the fact that the human body is incapable of making any minerals. Additionally, current soil cultivation methods are destroying farmlands of these valuable elements.

With all the mounting evidence that the old model of just three meals a day may not be providing you with enough protection to guard against possible mineral defi-ciencies, you may want to consider doing the following:

- Check with your health-care practitioner to assess your individual nutritional status.

- Make sure you follow the "Food Guide Pyramid" as closely as possible (see Figure 1.1 on page 19).

- Incorporate the use of a multi-vitamin and -mineral formula into your diet to hedge against possible nutri-tional deficiencies.

- Recheck your progress with your health-care profes-sional.

It is important to remember that a deficiency could be just a meal away!

After assessing the dynamic role minerals play in the maintenance and prolongation of many of the body's vital life processes, a key question may come to mind: If minerals float inactively in the bloodstream or are stored as inactive or inorganic elements in the body, how can they be powerful and how can a seemingly simple min-eral deficiency have such far-reaching implications on the preservation of health?

Read on! Chapter 2 will explain this phenomenon

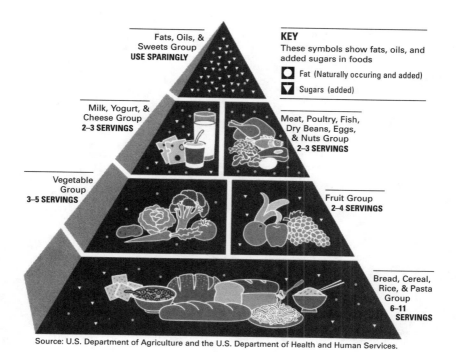

Source: U.S. Department of Agriculture and the U.S. Department of Health and Human Services.

Figure 1.1. The Food Guide Pyramid.

and show you just how these minerals change from an inorganic (nonliving) form to an organic (living) form capable of conducting electricity to initiate, control, and sustain many of the body's internal life processes.

2   ELECTROLYTES—
MINERALS ARE
ELECTRIC

All cellular structures become alive through electrolytic activity. Life begins with electrolytes while trace minerals carry the life force in our bodies more than any other substance.

—*Dr. Bernard Jensen, Ph.D., N.D.*
World-renowned author, scientist, and lecturer

Mineral electrolytes are vital to health and are the building blocks of life. An electrolyte is a substance whose molecules split into electrically charged particles called ions when melted or dissolved in water. The ions are then capable of conducting electricity. There are many ions that play important roles in regulating body processes. Some of these are potassium, sodium, calcium, magnesium, phosphorus, and chloride. When minerals become electrolytes, they become active and usable in human tissue. All cellular structures become alive through this electrolyte activity.

At the end of Chapter 1, a key question was posed: If minerals are classified as inorganic (nonliving) elements

21

and float inactively in the bloodstream, how can they initiate, control, and sustain many of the body's internal life processes? In essence, how can a nonliving element become alive and take part in the dynamic actions of living matter, as described by Dr. Jensen in the opening quote of this chapter? This chapter will answer that question.

ATOMS

Matter is defined as anything that occupies space and has weight. The basic component of matter is called the atom. According to researchers Buban and Schmitt, the atom is important to us because one of its parts is the electron. An atom is made of tiny particles known as electrons and protons. Electrons (which have negative charges) move about the center, or nucleus, of an atom in paths that are usually referred to as shells.

Each of these shells can contain only a certain maximum number of electrons. This number is called the "quota" of a shell. When every shell of the atom contains its quota of electrons, the atom is said to be in stable condition. The nucleus of the atom consists of particles called protons (which have positive charges) and neutrons (which have no charge, or are electrically neutral). All electrons are alike and all protons are alike. Therefore, atoms differ from one another only in the number of electrons and protons they contain.

ELEMENTS AND COMPOUNDS

When all the atoms within a substance are alike, that substance is called an element. All minerals are elements. Copper, iron, gold, carbon, and silicon are among the more than 100 different elements that are known to exist. Elements cannot be broken down into simpler sub-stances by normal means. Different elements can com-bine to form substances called compounds. Water, sugar, sulfuric acid, rubber, and plastic are examples of familiar compounds.

The smallest particle of a compound that has all the properties of that compound is called a molecule. A mol-ecule contains atoms of each of the elements that form the compound.

ENERGY LEVELS AND FREE ELECTRONS

The electrons in any given shell of an atom are said to be located at certain energy levels that are related to the dis-tance of the electrons from the nucleus of the atom. When external energy, such as heat, light, or electric energy, is applied to certain materials, the electrons with-in the atoms of these materials gain energy. This may cause the electrons to move to higher energy levels, that is, to move farther from the nuclei of their atoms.

When an electron has moved to the highest possible energy level (or the outermost shell of its atom), it is least attracted by the positive charges of the protons within the nuclei of their atoms. If enough energy is then applied to the atom, some of the electrons in the outer-most shell will leave the atom. These electrons are called free electrons.

IONS

Electrons and protons possess tiny amounts of electrical charges. Electrons have negative charges and protons have positive charges. The amount of the negative charge of each electron is equal to the amount of the pos-itive charge of each proton. It is the electrical attraction between these opposite charges that plays the essential role in holding the atom together.

Under normal conditions, the negative and positive charges within an atom are equal in value. The reason for this is that the atom contains an equal number of electrons and protons. An atom in this condition is said to be electrically neutral or in balance.

An ion is an electrically charged atom. If a neutral atom gains electrons, there are more electrons than protons within the atom, and it becomes a negatively charged ion. If a neutral atom loses electrons, protons outnumber the remaining electrons, and the atom becomes a positively charged ion. Ions with unlike charges attract one another; ions with like charges repel one another. The process by which atoms either gain or lose electrons is called ionization.

ELECTROLYTES IN THE BODY

The electrically charged particles formed during the process of ionization are called *electrolytes*. When in "solution" (body fluids and the bloodstream) or dissolved and transformed in water, ionic minerals become "alive." Without electrolytes, and the electricity they produce, life would be impossible.

Maintaining Fluid Balance

The electrolytes in the blood help move fluids into and out of the cells of the body. As long as the proper level of electrolytes is maintained in the blood, the proper fluids can be maintained throughout the body. This is called fluid and electrolyte balance.

Electrolyte balance can easily be disturbed by severe, excessive sweating, vomiting, or diarrhea. If this balance is disturbed, severe illness can result. For example, when water is lost in the intestinal tract due to diarrhea or vomiting, the body seeks to replenish this loss by drawing some of the water from between the cells. This area then tries to compensate for its loss by drawing out some of the cellular fluid. The kidneys then detect the loss and try to compensate by raising the levels of sodium outside the cells, which draws more water out of the cells, creating a vicious cycle. Without sufficient water the cells cannot function properly. This fluid and electrolyte imbalance can be life-threatening.

Maintaining Acid-Base Balance

Electrolytes in the blood also serve to maintain the acid-base balance (or pH balance) in the body. The blood is slightly basic—its pH range is 7.35 to 7.45 (a pH of 0 to 6.9 is acidic, 7 is neutral, and 7.1 to 14 is basic). It is very important that the blood's pH remains in this range because even the slightest change can severely affect several organs and can be life-threatening. There are several mechanisms that seek to maintain acid-base balance in the body. Minerals are among these mechanisms. Mineral salts (compounds created when positively charged and negatively charged ions are combined) act as *buffers* in the body's fluids. Buffers are compounds that neutralize acids or bases by collecting or releasing hydrogen ions, thereby maintaining the proper pH level.

Other Electrolyte Functions

Electrolytes also help maintain the proper volume of blood pumping through the arteries and veins, so that the blood pressure is adequate to circulate the blood to all parts of the body. Electrolytes in the body's fluids also act as carrying agents for amino acids and minerals. Electrolytes in the body need to be in balance for the system to function at full capacity. Electrolytes in the body's fluids are the electrical energy that keep the body functioning.

Dr. Alexis Carrel first demonstrated this remarkable principle when he kept a heart alive and beating for years outside the body in a solution containing the proper nutrients. Dr. George Crile, an early pioneer in discovering the healthy aspects of maintaining a proper balance of minerals in the system, stated that, "If we supply any cell with an electrolyte solution containing the essential chemicals and minerals, the cell can reestablish its electrical balance and return to health." Dr. Crile went on to say, "If we can do the same thing in the body as described above—feed cells the minerals they need to maintain their full electrical potential—then we have found the secret to health."

In many respects, the importance of minerals in initiating the electrolytic action of cellular structures in the body can be compared to the telephone system of the country. You want to communicate with a friend on the other coast, so you place the call. First, the "call" is translated into electrical impulses. These are sent to a major sending station that figures out the best and fastest way to transmit these impulses to their destination. At that destination, the impulses are then converted back to sound and the conversation takes place. There is no difficulty in understanding what is being said and everything is OK.

Now, imagine that in the transmission of your call, there was a big glitch at every station and telephone line around the country. In one area, the line was garbled because of bad weather, in another area of the country, a switchboard was defective, and someplace else, the power generator was working at only 90 percent of its power. Your conversation would be difficult and might never be completed if things got really bad. It's the same with minerals in your body. Minerals act as major transmission junctions and switches for the electrical message impulses that flow from the brain to the muscles. These impulses use the nervous system as transmission lines. The nervous system, like a telephone line, carries messages to and from the brain. The minerals are the switches that allow the electric impulses to flow without disruption or disturbance.

MAINTAINING ADEQUATE LEVELS OF ELECTROLYTES IN THE BODY

If you eat properly, with plenty of fruits and vegetables, then shouldn't you be getting enough electrolytes? Not necessarily. As you have learned, they may be lost quite easily due to profuse sweating, or severe vomiting or diarrhea. Drinking fluids with all the necessary electrolytes would be the best way to maintain the fluid and electrolyte balance.

Be aware that constant loss of vital mineral electrolytes can have severe negative consequences over the long run. You can, however, have your bloodstream levels of electrolytes checked in a simple lab blood test. This way, you can be certain that your electrolyte levels are balanced.

CONCLUSION

We now know that there are several factors involved with the proper utilization of mineral elements. Before minerals can do their jobs, they must be converted into a form that can interact with human tissue. Once minerals are transformed into ions, they are then able to conduct electricity and initiate their life-giving attributes.

Chapter 3 will explain another function of minerals that makes them necessary for life—their antioxidant abilities.

3 THE ANTIOXIDANT CONNECTION

During the 1980's, scientists discovered a strain of bacteria that could survive the lethal environment of radioactive waste water. One of the ways radioactivity kills most forms of life, including bacteria, is by releasing cascades of free radicals. But this particular bacterium generated high levels of antioxidants—as much as 50 times more than other bacteria—and was able to survive radiation.

—Dr. Robert D. Willix, Jr., M.D., open heart surgeon and author of "You Can Feel Good All the Time"

According to Dr. Robert Willix, M.D., who developed the first open-heart-surgery program in the state of South Dakota, antioxidants are the most important medical discovery in the last fifty years. He argues that the link between free radicals and the "aging disease" is the most important discovery since doctors learned that some illnesses are caused by germs. He went on to say that the germ theory of disease, set forth by Louis Pasteur over

100 years ago, has caused the eradication and controlled treatment of many diseases, such as smallpox, polio, tuberculosis, and rheumatic fever. But germs are no longer the big killers of our time. The big killers today are cancer, stroke, and heart disease. Our bodies today are wracked by allergies, arthritis, headaches, and chronic fatigue. These diseases are not caused by germs.

What causes the big killers of today? Just what are free radicals? What role do they play in disease initiation, activation, and acceleration? What are antioxidants? How do they work? Do any mineral elements have antioxidant capabilities?

This chapter will answer the above questions. It is concerned with the role of antioxidants, and the mineral elements with strong antioxidant properties. While free radicals, which are highly reactive molecules, are part of the normal metabolic process, uncontrolled free-radical aggression has been implicated as the cause of over sixty age-related degenerative diseases. Antioxidants, the body's natural guards against free radicals, can neutralize the harmful effects of these substances. This chapter will give a complete review of antioxidants and the role mineral elements have in promoting strong antioxidant reactions.

FREE RADICALS

The source of many degenerative diseases today are known as *free radicals*. Free radicals are atoms with an unpaired electron in their outer shells. Electrons normally exist in pairs, so free radicals are highly reactive with other molecules in their attempts to gain an electron, causing adverse chemical reactions in the body. Once they obtain an electron from another molecule, that molecule now becomes a free radical, seeking a molecule from which to obtain an electron, and a vicious and destructive cycle ensues.

Oxygen is a necessity for most animals and plants, but it can also be a poison. It is needed for the process of oxidation—a necessary process in which energy is freed from carbohydrates, fats, and proteins for use in the body. Unfortunately, even in the course of normal metabolism involving ordinary amounts of oxygen, harmful free radicals are created. Oxidation is what causes metal to rust or an apple to turn brown. Unstable oxygen molecules go to war in the body, grabbing onto other cells in their attempts to become stable.

Because our lives depend on very careful control of the chemical reactions within our bodies, free radicals can be deadly. Despite the fact that oxidation is one of the most necessary and fundamental biochemical reactions, not all oxidation is desirable. This uncontrolled phenomenon has been implicated in sixty age-related diseases.

Some free radicals are normal byproducts of metabolic reactions in the body, such as oxidation. But as you age, their numbers increase, and as they do, the chances also increase that these cellular saboteurs can do great harm, triggering inflammation and causing damage to blood vessels. Free radicals also attack cellular membranes, damaging them with sometimes drastic results. For example, lysosomes are particles within cells that contain powerful enzymes, which break down tissue constituents. When lysomal membranes are ruptured by free radicals, these enzymes are released, causing severe damage to surrounding tissues. Rheumatoid arthritis flares are caused by the above process.

The destruction that free radicals cause is the biological equivalent to a terrorist bomber going berserk in the control room of a nuclear reactor. The cumulative levels of oxidation caused by free radicals can put millions, even billions, of cells out of commission. According to Dr. Harry Demopoulos, coauthor of *Formula for Life: The Anti-Oxidant, Free-Radical Detoxification Program*, free-radical pathology is as important an advance in medicine as was Pasteur's germ theory of disease.

To contain the destructive cycle that free radicals cause, the body supplies enzymes that control them so they don't escape to do damage elsewhere. The enzymes superoxide dismutase (SOD) and glutathione peroxidase are two types of substances the body manufactures to control the subversive actions of free-radical molecules. Without these enzymes, you would quickly die. In fact, all air-breathing life forms on our planet must have such enzymes to survive.

Free-radical reactions have been investigated since the 1950s when Dr. Denham Harman first formulated the free-radical theory of aging. Dr. Harman suggested three methods of experimentally reducing free-radical damage in the bodies of experimental animals:

1. Reduce calories in the diet to reduce the production of free radicals during metabolism.

2. Minimize dietary components such as copper and polyunsaturated fats, which tend to increase free-radical production.

3. Add to the diet one or more free-radical quenchers, such as vitamins E, C, A, B_1, B_5, and B_6; the minerals zinc and selenium; and the amino acid cysteine.

As we have learned, the effectiveness of many of these enzyme-activated antioxidant systems are dependent on the level of mineral electrolytes present in the cell.

THE ROLE OF ANTIOXIDANTS

Free radicals are products of many normal and necessary metabolic reactions. Thus, all oxygen-using organisms have had to evolve defense mechanisms against free radicals. Antioxidants are the body's chief nutritional defense against the detrimental effects of free radicals. They do this by donating an electron to the free radical, minimizing its reactivity. Antioxidants, however, are able to maintain stability even after donating an electron, so they do not become free radicals themselves. Current investigations have revealed that it is also possible to prevent much of the damage caused by these highly destructive molecules by taking certain supplements.

Lester Packer, Ph.D., professor in the Department of Molecular and Cell Biology at the University of California at Berkeley, suggested that free radicals react readily with almost every cellular component and contribute to many types of disease. Packer said, "For example, if the [free-radical] target is DNA, the likelihood of cancer increases. If the target is low-density lipoprotein (LDL) in the blood, the likelihood of arteriosclerosis and cardiovascular disease increases. Additionally, free radicals attack and alter cell enzymes, the protein derived catalyst that speeds all metabolic processes. The damaged enzyme is inactivated, which slows or halts all processes dependent on that enzyme (including liberation of energy). Furthermore, these free radicals can activate dormant enzymes that in turn can cause tissue damage and diseases such as emphysema or can release neurotoxins that affect nerve and brain function."

Richard G. Cutler, Ph.D., of the Gerontology Research Center, National Institute of Aging in Baltimore, Maryland, states that "Oxidation may be a major cause of cell and tissue aging, no matter where it occurs in the body."

MINERALS AS ANTIOXIDANTS

The body has a fantastic ability to neutralize free radicals, which can be caused by normal metabolism, smoking, exercising, faulty digestive mechanisms, food additives, and degenerative diseases, as well as a host of other factors. It is when free radicals are produced faster than they are neutralized that serious damage can result. Antioxidants, such as vitamins C and E and beta-carotene, help the body neutralize free radicals by donating electrons without becoming free radicals themselves.

Scientists now know that minerals also play a vital role in this process of neutralization. Experimental evidence suggests that combined supplementation of selenium and vitamin E may help protect against tissue damage when there is insufficient blood flow and, hence, too little oxygen supply to an organ. Angina sufferers who received 1 milligram (1,000 micrograms) of selenium and 200 international units of vitamin E per day experienced considerable relief from the excruciating chest pain that characterizes this heart condition.

Studies have also shown that the mineral zinc is vital to the role of superoxide dismutase (SOD). SOD is a powerful defender against free radicals because it destroys superoxide molecules, one of the most common free radicals in the body. In fact, SOD cannot function without zinc. A recent study at the University of California showed that zinc monomethionine, a zinc supplement, reduces excess levels of superoxide free radicals produced by white blood cells.

MINERAL BALANCING

Minerals serve another essential function in their roles as antioxidants. They can help regulate the speed of oxidation in the body. Oxidation is the process by which certain elements in the body chemically combine with oxygen to release energy. A person can be a fast, slow, mixed, or normal oxidizer. If both the thyroid and adrenal glands are overactive, a person will be a "fast oxidizer." This person functions at high speeds until he or she suddenly collapses. On the other hand, when both glands are underactive, a person will be a "slow oxidizer." This person can be oversensitive, anxious, or emotionally evasive. However, if one of these glands is overactive and the other is underactive, a person will be a "mixed oxidizer" and will be on an energy roller coaster. Carla Cassata, a health educator and iridologist who has studied with the renowned Dr. Bernard Jensen, has reported that each of the above routes leads to premature aging and premature death. She went on to say that in her research, she has found that the "balanced oxidizer" is happy, content, and open and possesses an inner calm and steadiness. This person is also the most powerful and productive type of person.

The ultimate goal of mineral supplementation is to bring the body into a state of balanced oxidation by balancing the mineral levels in the bloodstream. Numerous minerals, including calcium, magnesium, sodium, potassium, iron, copper, zinc, molybdenum, and boron, are involved in this process. The importance of maintaining this balancing act is crucial, as expressed by Dr. Paul Eck, a scientist and renowned mineral researcher from Phoenix, Arizona. Dr. Eck claims that the slow oxidizer actually dies from mineral accumulation, while the fast oxidizer dies from mineral bankruptcy. In fact, it has been reported in the *Eck Institute Healthview Newsletter* that 95 percent of the people who die, do so as slow oxidizers.

CONCLUSION

Free radicals are part of our lives and in many cases are involved in or are the result of normal metabolism, including digestion. They have been implicated as a major cause of heart disease, arthritis, Alzheimer's disease, and cancer.

While there has been much media attention focused on the popular vitamin supplements, such as vitamins A, C, E, and beta-carotene, it is important to remember that these substances cannot function unless their partners, namely minerals, are present. Besides being the biochemical catalysts that put the antioxidant capabilities of other nutrients into motion, minerals have strong antioxidant capabilities of their own. Because of the factors cited above, it would be wise to make sure your antioxidant regimen is backed by a complete mineral formula.

Chapter 4 will take a look at the several different types of mineral supplements and the formulations in which they can be found.

4 THE ABSORPTION PROBLEM

There is some evidence that the problem of absorption of some chelated minerals is improved. The process may be facilitated further if the supplement is "hydrolyzed," meaning it dissolves more easily in water.

—Dr. Michael Colgan, Ph.D., C.C.N., founder, Colgan Nutritional Institute; council member, International and American Association of Clinical Nutritionists

What factors affect the availability of minerals to the body? What are the different forms mineral supplements can be found in? What is the best way to obtain minerals? What is chelation? Does chelation enhance absorption rates of minerals?

This chapter seeks to answer the above questions. We will also take a look at the various methods scientists have come up with to enhance absorption of mineral supplements.

HOW ABSORPTION WORKS

Once minerals are consumed, they must still be absorbed into the bloodstream in order to be utilized by the body. Once food is taken into the body, it is first chewed in the mouth, it then travels down the esophagus and into the stomach where it is further broken down a bit. From the stomach, swallowed food travels to the small intestine. It is here that nutrient absorption takes place.

The inside of the small intestine is lined with tiny fingerlike projections called villi. The villi increase the surface area of the small intestine. There are blood vessels running through the villi. As food passes through the small intestine, the nutrients attach to receptors on the villi, pass through its cells, are absorbed into the blood vessels, and enter the bloodstream.

FACTORS THAT AFFECT MINERAL ABSORPTION

It is not enough to simply obtain enough minerals in the diet. There are several factors in the body that determine how much of the available mineral is actually absorbed into the bloodstream and used in the body.

Age

While aging is a natural process, it causes a slow-down of many of our internal metabolic and digestive processes. Our ability to properly absorb and use nutrients is diminished with age. Aging can have a negative impact on the way our bodies handle the breakdown of minerals. As we grow older, it becomes more and more important to ensure that we use mineral supplements in the most absorbable forms.

Pregnancy and Lactation

Pregnancy and lactation can have quite an impact on the way that our bodies absorb ingested minerals into the bloodstream. While a woman is pregnant or breast-feeding, her body's nutritional demands are needed not only to support her life process but also her developing fetus or her breastfeeding infant. For these reasons, a pregnant or breastfeeding woman's mineral absorption is increased. These mothers must increase their intake of minerals (and all nutrients) during these time periods.

Defective Enzymes

Enzymes are the body's labor force. They help keep many reactions and internal processes going. When enzyme function is compromised, metabolic processes slow down. Without the proper function of enzymes, the digestive process does not take place adequately. Enzymes break down foods for proper digestion. If food is not digested properly, its minerals cannot be extracted and absorbed into the bloodstream.

A Person's Biochemical Make-Up

Certain hereditary or genetic disorders can impede or increase nutrient absorption. For example, pernicious anemia occurs due to a deficiency of what is called intrinsic factor. Without this intrinsic factor, the body is unable to absorb vitamin B_{12}, and thus cobalt. The genetic disorder hemochromatosis is a potentially fatal disorder in which sufferers accumulate an excessive amount of iron in their cells, which can damage the liver, heart, and pancreas.

There are several other factors that can impede mineral absorption, including the overconsumption of alcohol, the use of certain drugs, autoimmune diseases, allergies, pH imbalances, radiation, and electrolyte imbalance.

NEW APPROACHES TO MINERAL SUPPLEMENTATION

One of the major problems in human nutrition is increasing the bioavailability of nutrients. Bioavailability is the degree to which a nutrient is available for absorption by the body. The nutrient content of the food we eat and the way in which our bodies absorb, store, and use those nutrients is vital to our health. Drs. Arnold and Barry Fox, an internist and a cardiologist practicing in Beverly Hills, California, are working on a new frontier in nutrition called nutrition testing. Together, they are determining how well nutrients are being used by the body. The test, which is called Essential Metabolic Analysis (EMA), does not measure the levels of the nutrients available for cells to use. Instead, EMA determines how well nutrients function within the cells. These two pioneers claim that just putting enough food on the table doesn't guarantee that cells can and will use the nutrients properly.

The way nutrients, especially minerals, are absorbed and handled by the body has and continues to be a main concern of researchers. Many minerals that get into the system pass right out the body without being utilized because the particles are just too large to be absorbed. Investigations into this problem have shown that absorption of certain nutritional minerals in the human gastrointestinal (GI) tract depends, in large part, on their chemical form. In recent years, significant advances in our understanding of the bioavailability of minerals has given rise to a new generation of mineral supplements. Some of these forms of mineral supplements include chelated minerals, minerals in colloidal dispersion, and crystalloid minerals.

Chelated Minerals

When a mineral is chelated, it has been combined with another substance, usually an amino acid, to enhance absorption. The amino acid transports the mineral to the absorption site—the upper part of the small intestine. Here, the mineral can be absorbed into the bloodstream where it can be utilized.

There are many forms of mineral chelates available today. The three basic categories are:

- Inorganic mineral salts.

- Organic mineral chelates.

- Full-range amino-acid chelates.

Each is manufactured differently, resulting in varying degrees of absorption.

Inorganic Mineral Salts

Mineral salts are compounds formed when a positively charged mineral ion (or a base or a metal) is combined with a negatively charged ion (or an acid or a nonmetal) in order to enhance absorption. Some mineral salts include oxides, phosphates, and carbonates. The problem with supplemental mineral salts is that they are negatively charged, as is the intestine. The like charges make absorption of the mineral difficult. Consequently, the majority of the mineral passes through the intestines unabsorbed.

Organic Mineral Chelates

The chelating agents in organic mineral chelates are taken from plant or animal sources. Some include fumarates, gluconates, citrates, and commonly available forms of amino-acid chelates. Mixed in solution, organic chelates are more stable as they surround the mineral, which helps prevent the breakdown of the chelate in the stomach.

Although all of the above organic chelated minerals can be somewhat effective, the pH range of the supplement is important in determining its effectiveness. A pH (which stands for potential hydrogen) level is a measure of the acidity or alkalinity of a substance. It is measured on a scale ranging from 0 to 14. A pH of 0 to 6.9 is considered acid, 7 is neutral, and 7.1 to 14 is alkaline. The most effective form of chelation possible would be one with a neutral pH. The closer the amino acid chelate is to a neutral pH, the stronger the bond between the amino acid and the mineral.

Full-Range Amino-Acid Chelates

To prepare a full-range amino-acid chelate, a protein molecule is broken down in a solution to form short chains of amino acids. Then the mineral desired to be chelated is separated from its salt by ionization in solution. These solutions are then reacted together under favorable chemical conditions, to form a full-range amino-acid chelate. This process ensures that the mineral is completely surrounded by the chelate, which more completely protects the mineral from destruction in the gastrointestinal tract. Full-range amino-acid chelates have a pH of 5 or more and have a neutral or slightly negative charge. These factors make full-range amino-acid chelates the strongest and most stable amino-acid chelate possible, as well as the most absorbable mineral form because it is so easily transported through the intestinal wall into the bloodstream.

Liquid Mineral Supplements

All substances found in the universe are composed of chemicals and exist in one of three possible states: gas, liquid, or solid. For example, water exists as a solid when frozen into ice, as a liquid in its drinkable form, and as a gas when boiled into steam.

Matter in various states may be mixed together. For example, dust particles (solids) may be suspended in water (liquid) or in the air (gas). Such mixtures are called suspensions. They are not permanent mixtures because the particles are so large and heavy that they settle out in time.

Another type of mixture is called a solution. In such a mixture, the particles, or molecules, of the solid are small enough to become uniformly distributed among the molecules of a liquid, such as water. They form a homogeneous mixture that does not separate out. Take the mixture of sugar and water for example. The sugar, called the solute is said to dissolve in the water, called the solvent. Water can dissolve thousands of chemicals, and forms the basic medium of living matter. Liquids and gases, such as oxygen, can also form solutions in water or in other liquids.

In nature, minerals are often found in solutions or suspensions in water. Since they are found this way in nature, many scientists contend that this is the best form in which to take mineral supplements.

Supplement manufacturers now formulate mineral supplements in liquid form. Liquid mineral supplements more closely resemble the form in which minerals occur in nature. They are the most absorbable type of mineral supplement—99- to 100-percent absorbable. Most minerals can be bought in liquid form. Liquid mineral supplements can be found in the same formulations as tablets—salts, chelates, multimineral formulations, and individual mineral supplements—and can generally be found in the same stores. If you have any problems finding them, check your local health-food store. If you still have problems finding liquid mineral supplements, you can contact the manufacturers directly and order their products through the mail. See Appendix A for a list of manufacturers of liquid mineral supplements. Because of their superior formulation, liquid mineral supplements are more expensive than minerals in tablet form, but remember—you get what you pay for.

Colloidal Dispersions

A colloidal dispersion lies somewhere between a suspension and a solution. It is similar to a solution, except the particles of the dispersed substance are larger so they do not become completely invisible in the mixture. Minerals sold in colloidal dispersions are dispersed in water. The minute mineral substances remain dispensed in a liquid medium because of their size and their electrical charges.

Some researchers contend that colloidal minerals are better because they more closely resemble the colloidal dispersions present in the body's own cells. Accordingly, they are thought to be small enough to allow direct entry into the system for greater delivery and more bioavailability. However, researchers Ward and Hertzel, authors of *Biology Today and Tomorrow*, state that in "colloid mixtures, the particles are too large and do not dissolve." Also, data found in organic chemistry revealed that colloidal particles are too large to pass through a living membrane and are incapable of passing through the cells' semipermeable membranes.

Additionally, Callewaert and Genyea state that the dispersed substance in a colloid may exist as individual macromolecules (large molecules), and more often as accumulations of many smaller particles, both of which may hamper the ability of the minerals to pass through the cell membranes. These researchers argue that these clumps are formed either by breaking up larger pieces of a substance or by causing a large number of individual small molecules to clump together.

Furthermore, if the concentration of a colloidal solution is too high, there is more of a tendency for the particles to collide into each other, resulting in the particles becoming too large and settling out of the solution, thus needing to be shaken or have stabilizers added. This pattern, which does not occur in true solutions, is known as Brownian motion. Data shows that the Brownian motion keeps particles of colloidal size from settling out but will not prevent the settling of larger particles.

Crystalloids

Without water, there would be no blood, lymph, digestive juices, urine, sweat, or tears—there would be no life. Our bodies use water as a solvent to transport nutrients. Water comes close to being the universal solvent. The water of the earth has been found to contain about one-half of all known elements. It is an inert solvent, meaning that the water itself is not chemically changed by the compounds it dissolves, thereby enabling it to be used over and over again. Emphasizing the importance of this property of solubility is the fact that the roots of plants can only absorb nutrients in solution and our human food must be dissolved in a solution before it can enter the bloodstream.

Nature converts inorganic minerals like colloidals into a useable form for us through water that flows and swirls over rocks. This action picks up minerals as it rushes over soil and cascades over rocks. This occurrence produces vortices (whirling masses of fluid, not unlike a tornado or whirlpool). Research has shown that these vortex patterns make possible the transformation of minerals, wherein they change from a colloidal form (which is too large to penetrate cell membranes) to a crystalloid one, which readily passes through the cell wall.

Crystalloids are substances like crystals that form a true solution and can pass through a semipermeable membrane. This breakthrough information was first investigated by Louis Kervan in his book *Biological Transmutations*. Kervan was an active member of the New York Academy of Sciences and a French researcher in chemistry and biochemistry.

As mentioned in Chapter 2, minerals that are broken down into their smallest ionic state and then put into water will break down into a solution that can be assimilated by the human body. Also, when water is removed from a solution of ionic minerals, the minerals will combine and organize into crystals, going from a state of disorganization to an organized state.

New data suggests that any other forms of mineral will not even go into a true solution with water, making them very difficult to assimilate in the body. Some of the mineral particles might float or suspend in the water, but those particles would be too large to pass through the semipermeable membrane of the cell wall. They will not conduct or produce energy, and when the water is removed, they will not crystallize.

During the process of osmosis (the process by which minerals penetrate cell membranes), crystalloid minerals are electrically charged and found in the solution. As such, they form true electrolytes. This form of mineral bypasses the digestive system and is available for immediate use by the cells, providing the electrical energy necessary to run the organism. As such, it is assimilated 100 percent by the body.

Based upon current data, I would highly recommend the crystalloid form of minerals over other forms for supplementation. It is the most absorbable form of mineral supplement and the most bioavailable to the body once it is absorbed into the bloodstream. If you are unable to find crystalloid liquid mineral supplements, mineral supplements in a colloidal dispersion are the next best thing. Minerals in both crystalloid and colloidal forms are more expensive than the more familiar tablets, but you usually have to pay more for better quality.

Water

Charles B. Ahlson, the late expert on the value of sea water, wrote, "Remember, all minerals are in sea water in almost direct proportion to the mineral content of our bloodstream." However, today, in this era of environmental pollution, soil and waterways have become widely contaminated with heavy metals. Also, food processing destroys many valuable nutrients. To add to these problems, the water that comes through our taps today is also highly processed, with mineral content altered and chemicals added. Additionally, distilled water or artificially softened water has had practically all minerals removed. While softened water may be preferred for cleaning purposes, scientists agree that when mineral-free water is consumed, it leaches out of the body what minerals already exist there. This is apparently due to an ion exchange within the body through the membranes. In other words, consuming excessive amounts of mineral-free water can result in mineral imbalances.

Hard water contains minerals. Soft water either contains very few minerals or has had the minerals removed from it. The more minerals in the water, the harder the water. The fewer the minerals, the softer the water. In a study of seventy-six communities in Sweden, there was an association between water hardness and death from ischemic heart disease (IHD—restriction of blood flow) and stroke. Those with softer water had a 41-percent higher mortality rate from IHD and a 14-percent higher rate from stroke than those with harder water.

A large body of research suggests that magnesium, calcium, zinc, copper, chromium, selenium, and other trace minerals are protective against cardiovascular disease. Nevertheless, it seems unlikely that the concentration of these minerals in the drinking water alone could explain as much as a 41 percent difference in IHD mortality. Water is a relatively insignificant source of minerals, the bulk of which are obtained from food. On second glance, however, the results of this study may not be so farfetched. Minerals dissolved in water may be considerably more bioavailable than those present in food, because they are already in solution. This study suggests that mineral bioavability may be more important than the absolute amount of minerals in the diet.

Dr. John Sorenson, a medical chemist and professor at the University of Arkansas, whose specialty is the properties of and the metabolism of inorganic materials, states, "Mineral absorption is greater from drinking water than from food. . . . For gastric intestinal absorption, things in solution are well absorbed simply because water is well absorbed, [so] anything in it would also be."

Because of the above factors, many researchers believe that it may be more beneficial for optimum health to get minerals dissolved in liquid.

CONCLUSION

Based on current data, it may be wise to consider the overall benefits of getting your minerals via liquid mineral supplementation. As stated by Dr. John Sorenson, mineral bioavailability is greatly increased when drinking them in liquid form rather than relying solely on food sources. Furthermore, due to the fact that studies have shown that absorption of certain mineral elements is determined in large part by their chemical form, it is advisable to utilize liquid.

To offset any possible leaching of valuable mineral stores, health officials maintain that home water supplies should be tested for hardness or softness. When water is soft, it is considered to be void of valuable mineral elements. Hard water contains more of these essential nutrients. Studies have revealed that hard water has the capacity to reduce ischemic heart disease.

Even if you do ingest "enough" minerals, numerous factors can inhibit proper absorption of these minerals into the bloodstream. To tip the scales in your favor, liquid mineral supplementation is strongly advised.

This brings Part One to a close. Thus far, we have looked at the nature of minerals and their roles as biological catalysts. In Part Two, we will examine the individual attributes of the minerals that are absolutely essential to normal cell function.

PART TWO

THE
INDIVIDUAL MINERALS

In Part One, we examined the roles of minerals in our bodies and in our health. In Part Two, we will look at the attributes of the individual minerals. The macro minerals will be discussed first in alphabetical order, immediately followed by the micro minerals. For each mineral, I will explain the value that it has in our bodies, its recommended dosage, its food sources, the effects of a deficiency, how much is too much and what effect this overdose may have in the body, and the recommended form in which to take it. All of this information will be valuable in helping you establish a program for balancing mineral levels in your body for optimum health.

5   CALCIUM

Calcium is the most abundant mineral in the body. A 150-pound body contains about 2.2 pounds of calcium. About 99 percent of the calcium in the body is in the bones and in the teeth.

ROLES IN THE BODY

Adequate development and maintenance of bones and teeth are dependent on calcium absorption and metabolism. The remaining one percent (ten grams, or about two-thirds of a tablespoon) is essential for many vital functions, such as:

- Blood clot formation.

- Muscle contraction and growth.

- Transmission of nerve impulses.

- Absorption of vitamin B_{12}.

- Serving as a metabolic cofactor for many reactions.

- Controlling the concentration of many substances on either side of the cell membrane.

- Releasing energy from macronutrients (carbohydrates, fat, and protein).

- Maintaining rhythmic heart action.

- Preventing the accumulation of too much acid alkali in the blood.

- Aiding in the body's utilization of iron.

Phosphorus has been found to increase the absorption and utilization of calcium. Calcium and phosphorus should probably be taken in a 2 to 1 ratio. You must be careful to be sure that you do not take in more phosphorus than you do calcium, as too much phosphorus has been found to inhibit the absorption of calcium.

More than half of the calcium found in blood is ionized (having a positive or negative electrical charge). The remaining calcium is bound to protein. The protein bound with calcium acts as a weak electrolyte. The metabolically available ionized calcium is found in soft tissue, extra cellular fluid, and blood. It is the ionized form that is active in all aspects of calcium metabolism.

Calcium and Osteoporosis

Numerous scientific studies have confirmed that calcium helps slow down the development of osteoporosis, the disease of weakened and brittle bones. Postmenopausal women need more of this nutrient than the Recommended Dietary Allowances (about 1,000 milligrams) because their bodies' natural calcium-absorbing abilities diminish as they get older. Investigations at the University of California, San Diego, have positively correlated sufficient calcium intake (especially during pre-menopausal years) with increased bone density in post-menopausal women. Additionally, calcium supplementation can greatly reduce the possibility of fractures in postmenopausal women

One of the keys to preventing the onset of osteoporosis, especially in women, is to follow a daily regimen of calcium consumption and/or supplementation. Current data from new research by pediatrician Steven A. Abrams at the Children's National Research Center in Houston, Texas shows that this regimen is critical, especially between the ages of five and ten.

According to Dr. Abrams, it is crucial that adequate dosages be maintained during the years before eleven years of age to prevent bone-crippling osteoporosis in old age. His research confirms the fact that most bone-forming activities occur in the years just before and just after the start of puberty, which on average is age ten. Menstruation usually occurs two or three years later, and by age fifteen, most bone-forming activity has stopped. In his opinion, the higher the bone mass at this stage, the lower the odds of having osteoporosis later in life.

Previously, researchers had reported that drinking coffee increases urinary loss of minerals such as calcium and iron, which can increase a woman's risk for developing osteoporosis or anemia. A recent study by the Mayo Clinic in Rochester reports that coffee, or more specifically caffeine, does not appear to pose a risk for young women. However, high caffeine intake in older women who already show signs of a calcium deficiency could make these women prone to developing osteoporosis.

Other Functions

Casoni and coworkers found that calcium along with

magnesium is directly responsible for activating the mechanisms in muscle contractions.

Researchers now know that magnesium also plays an integral part as a primary regulator of calcium flow within cells. This delicate collaboration may be the major determinant of the rate at which the cellular flames burn. Calcium and magnesium should, therefore, be taken in a 2 to 1 ratio to increase calcium's absorption and utilization. Additionally, besides providing structure and strength to skeletal tissue, calcium plays a major role in proper nerve function and the transmission of nerve impulses. The neurotransmitters affected by calcium are serotonin, acetylcholine, and norepinephrine. Neurotransmitters found in the brain can be compared to your television station, which insures proper transmission signals. Neurotransmitters insure that the brain signals are properly communicating.

RECOMMENDED DOSAGES AND TOXICITY LEVELS

The U.S. Recommend Dietary Allowance (RDA) for calcium is 1,000 milligrams; however, Dr. Kenneth Cooper, a noted researcher and author of *Preventing Osteoporosis*, maintains that women should take about 1,500 milligrams of calcium daily. I recommend this dosage as well. Women over fifty may need 2,000 milligrams per day. Ask your doctor.

Calcium has no known toxic effects. It was once thought that high intakes of calcium were connected with the development of kidney stones; however, this does not seem to be the case. In fact, researchers now believe that a lot of calcium in the diet may even reduce the risk associated with kidney stone formation.

In a recent study, 45,000 men between the ages of 40

and 75 were evaluated to determine the correlation between calcium intake and the formation of kidney stones. A four-year follow-up of the subjects revealed that calcium intake actually helped to inhibit stone formation. They found that it was the men who had a high intake of animal protein and a reduced potassium and water intake who were more susceptible to developing kidney stones.

FOOD SOURCES

Milk and dairy products, dark green vegetables, and dried legumes are good sources of calcium. All raw nuts also contain calcium, as do raw sesame seeds, which contain more calcium than any other food on earth. Most fruits contain ample amounts of calcium, particularly strawberries, elderberries, dates, dried apricots, raisins, and oranges.

SUPPLEMENTS

Calcium supplements can be found in tablet, liquid, capsule, caplet, and powder formulations. Some common forms of calcium supplements include calcium carbonate, calcium citrate, calcium citrate malate, calcium gluconate, calcium hydroxyapatite, and calcium lactate. It can also be found as bone meal and dolomite (a combination of calcium and magnesium) and chelated with proteins.

I recommend the use of calcium citrate and calcium citrate malate. These forms are highly absorbable and require minimal hydrochloric acid for absorption. These forms are excellent for the elderly, who tend to have more gastrointestinal disorders and low levels of hydrochloric acid, both of which can inhibit absorption.

Test Your Calcium Supplement's Absorbability at Home

Dr. Robert Heany, a professor at Creighton University and a noted calcium expert, argues that "many of the generic brand supplements are so badly formulated, they don't disintegrate adequately." In other words, they are not bioavailable.

To test your supplement, Dr. Paul Miller, an associate clinical professor of medicine at the University of Colorado Health Sciences Center School of Medicine in Denver, suggests dropping two of your calcium tablets in six ounces of vinegar. Wait thirty minutes, stirring every two to three minutes. "If the tablets break up into small fragments, it's probably dissolving well in the stomach."

For pharmacological testing of the dissolution of calcium supplements and/or ability of the body to absorb them, scientists must use standards and guidelines as outlined in a manual called "U.S. Pharmacopeia."

Calcium gluconate, protein chelates, and calcium hydroxyapatite are also good forms. I would stay away from calcium carbonate and dolomite, however, as neither is very well absorbed, and dolomite may contain unacceptable levels of lead. Bone meal should also be avoided due to its high phosphorus content.

Many take antacids as a source of calcium. This is not a good idea, since many products contain aluminum. The aluminum could actually inhibit calcium absorption. Elevated bloodstream levels of aluminum have also been implicated as a causative factor in the development of Alzheimer's disease.

When buying a multimineral formula, be sure that the calcium and phosphorus in the supplement are in a two to one ratio in your supplement. Many suggest that you take your calcium supplement on an empty stomach, since hydrochloric acid is necessary for the absorption of calcium, and many may be deficient in hydrochloric acid. This way, your stomach does not have to work as hard breaking down other food material.

6   CHLORIDE

When chlorine combines with another mineral, it is called chloride. This is the form in which it is useful to the body. Chloride accounts for about 3 percent of the body's total mineral count and comprises 0.15 percent of body weight, but it aids in both digestion and metabolism. It is mainly a part of body fluids outside the cells. It is responsible for helping to control water and acid-base balance and fluid pressure in the body. It is a constituent of gastric juices, and as such, functions as an activator of amylases (enzymes that break down starch). It is found in virtually all our food.

Chloride also helps stimulate the liver to function as a filter for wastes, aids in keeping joints and tendons in youthful shape, helps to distribute hormones, and assists in hair and teeth growth.

Chloride is readily and almost completely absorbed in the gastrointestinal tract. Factors affecting sodium loss (vomiting, diarrhea, sweating) will similarly affect chloride output. The highest body concentrations are stored in the cerebrospinal fluid and in the gastrointestinal tract. Chloride should not be confused with chlorine, a highly poisonous gas. The chlorine used to disinfect water is an activated form of chloride with no nutritional value.

RECOMMENDED DOSAGES, TOXICITY LEVELS, AND FOOD SOURCES

We get chloride from table salt, and since most Americans use too much salt, chloride is unnecessary in supplements. The safe level of intake of chloride for adults is 750 milligrams. Ingested amounts exceeding 750 milligrams will cause symptoms of toxicity, including headaches, dizziness, confusion, and irritability. It should be noted that the toxic effects of sodium chloride are caused by the sodium and not the chloride.

SUPPLEMENTS

Chloride may be found in some multimineral formulas in very small dosages. Individual chloride supplements are not readily found in stores and should be avoided.

7   MAGNESIUM

Magnesium is an essential mineral that accounts for about 0.05 percent of body weight, equaling about 20 to 28 grams. Approximately 60 to 65 percent of the body's magnesium content is found in bones, and 27 percent originates in muscle. Magnesium is absolutely essential for life, as it is part of every major biological process, including the metabolism of glucose, the production of cellular energy, and the synthesis of nucleic acids and other proteins. Nucleic acids are molecular substances, such as DNA (deoxyribonucleic acid), found in the nuclei of all cells. Nucleic acids carry the cell's genetic code. This genetic code is unique and can be thought of as a specific combination used to formulate you and your physical characteristics.

ROLES IN THE BODY

This mighty mineral promotes the absorption of other minerals, including calcium, phosphorus, sodium, and potassium. Additionally, magnesium aids amino-acid synthesis, lipid (fat) metabolism, thiamine (vitamin B_1) utilization, neuromuscular transmission, and other enzymatic reactions. Furthermore, in controlled studies of rats, investigators found that magnesium prevented calcium deposits, kidney stones, and gallstones. Magnesium is also used regularly in hospital emergency rooms for heart attack victims to help control any damage caused by the heart attack.

Magnesium and the Heart

Epidemiological (disease) studies suggest that the death rate from ischemic heart disease (a deficiency of blood to the heart) is increased in areas with soft water. Soft water does not contain magnesium and calcium, as hard water does. According to M.S. Seeling, as reported by Sheldon Saul Hendler, coauthor of *The Complete Guide to Anti-Aging Nutrients*, magnesium is the more important factor in the protection against ischemic heart disease.

Dr. Sherry Rogers, M.D., who specializes in treating the undiagnosable and incurable, declares that there are nutrients that accomplish the same functions in the body as nearly every drug. Magnesium, she believes, can be as effective as, if not more effective than, several heart medications, and its use can save several lives.

Results of a United States government survey revealed that 40 percent of the American public does not get the magnesium they need daily. Studies in cardiology journals show that of those who enter the emergency room suffering from heart attacks, the major difference between those who walk out and those who do not is the amount of magnesium in their bloodstreams. Those with higher levels of magnesium in their bloodstreams are more likely to survive. Other studies have shown that if an injection of magnesium is given as soon as the patient arrives in the emergency room, this action more than doubles the patient's chance of survival. Yet, this is not a routine procedure.

A *Journal of the American Medical Association (J.A.M.A.)* article confirms this fact. When a group of researchers studied 1,033 patients in a hospital, they found that 54 percent of those patients with heart problems were low in magnesium. Many of these patients died of magnesium-deficiency related symptoms. The worst fact in this *J.A.M.A.* study was that 90 percent of the physicians never even ordered a magnesium test.

Current data has shown that magnesium has a direct effect on the maintenance of the electrical and physical integrity of heart muscle. One of the causes of ischemic heart disease occurs when coronary arteries fail to provide all of the oxygen necessary for proper heart function, thus causing spasmatic interruptions. Seeling maintains that Western diets are problematic in that they don't provide adequate magnesium levels, which may be the cause of the high rates of cardiovascular disease in Western nations, especially among men.

Excessive losses or diminished intakes of magnesium can cause potentially fatal disruptions of normal cardiac rhythm (a condition known as cardiac dysrhythmia), causing a heart attack. Iseri and coworkers have successfully treated ventricular dysrhythmias with magnesium. Although in their experiments normal blood level ranges of this mineral existed, they found deficiencies at the cellular level. This phenomenon's existence had also been demonstrated by researchers Cohen and Kitzes.

As discussed earlier, scientists are now studying how cells are utilizing nutrients once inside the cell, rather than just testing blood serum levels of a nutrient, via a new testing procedure called the Essential Metabolic Analysis. As suggested, the cellular measure is much more reliable and should be used more often, especially when dealing with patients on diuretics and digitalis (a heart medication), both of which are known to cause diminished magnesium levels. According to researchers Pike and Brown, "Whatever the nutritional potential of an element or food, that contribution is nonexistent if it isn't absorbed." These researchers declared that "nutrients that never penetrate through the intestinal muscosal cell to enter the circulation, for all nutritional intent and purposes, have never been eaten or utilized."

Premenstrual Syndrome (PMS)

In a study conducted by doctors from the Royal Sussex Country Hospital in Brighton, low levels of magnesium were related to the symptoms of premenstrual syndrome (PMS). This study was stimulated by research carried out in the United States by Dr. G. E. Abraham, who first suggested that many of the diverse symptoms of PMS might be due to a deficiency of magnesium. Studies suggest that some women who suffer from premenstrual syndrome have low blood levels of magnesium due to improper eating habits. This correlates with similar actions and reactions of a magnesium deficiency, such as muscle cramps, mood swings, and appetite changes. Conversely, some researchers believe that variations in estrogen levels speed up marginal magnesium deficiencies and their problematic manifestations.

Kidney Stones

Evidence suggests that magnesium is effective in counteracting calcium-oxalate stones in certain people susceptible to its recurrence. Doses of 200 milligrams of magnesium daily supplemented with 10 milligrams of vitamin B_6 proved to be effective. Other studies have shown that 300 milligrams of magnesium oxide daily also eliminated concurrent episodes of this malady.

Energy

Magnesium is essential to all energy-dependent reactions in the body, including the use and manufacture of adenosine triphosphate (ATP). ATP is a compound found in all cells. It produces energy for all cells for several bodily processes including the metabolism of certain nutrients and muscle contraction. All of our metabolic pathways depend upon the energy produced by ATP. Also, in a study conducted at Southhampton General Hospital, Southhampton, United Kingdom, patients suffering from chronic fatigue syndrome who were treated with magnesium had improved energy levels and emotional states.

Blood Pressure

Higher magnesium levels in the body have also been found to help normalize blood pressure levels. Dr. Eric Trimmer, editor of *The British Journal of Clinical Practice,* reminds us that when the body's magnesium level supply decreases—for example, when body fluids are lost due to severe gastroenteritis—there is a sudden rise in blood pressure. Conversely, according to Dr. Trimmer, if large doses of magnesium are given to patients with a severe degree of hypertension, blood pressure is lowered quite rapidly.

Blood Sugar

As we age, our bodies can have a diminished capacity to

efficiently handle blood sugar. A condition known as insulin resistance develops that corresponds with elevated blood sugar levels. Researchers at the University of Naples in Italy reported that magnesium supplementation in older individuals improves insulin resistance, which might help prevent the development of diabetes. These researchers recommended an intake of 350 milligrams to 450 milligrams of magnesium daily.

Other Functions in the Body

Magnesium has several other roles in the body.

- It is necessary for strong bones.
- It is interrelated with vitamin C metabolism.
- It promotes elimination.
- It exerts a quieting action on neuromuscular irritability.
- It is involved in energy production.
- It is needed for healthy muscle tone.
- It prevents the building up of cholesterol.
- It acts as a natural tranquilizer.
- It regulates acid-alkaline balance in the system.

RECOMMENDED DOSAGES

The National Research Council recommends a daily intake of 350 milligrams for the adult male and 300 milligrams for the adult female. I recommend that adult men and women take 700 milligrams of magnesium daily for optimum health. Studies have shown that the painful uterine contractions experienced by women toward the end of pregnancy could result from a deficiency of magnesium.

FOOD SOURCES

Much of our food is deficient in magnesium because of added chemicals and refining processes. Beans, bran, Brussels sprouts, clams, corn, nuts, oatmeal, prunes, raisins, and whole grains are good sources of magnesium.

SUPPLEMENTS

Magnesium can be found in such forms as magnesium aspartate, magnesium oxide, magnesium carbonate, and magnesium citrate, as well as protein chelates. I generally recommend the aspartate and citrate forms, as they are better absorbed. While there is more elemental magnesium present in the carbonate and oxide forms, they are not as well absorbed.

When taking individual magnesium supplements, do not take them with or immediately following a meal, as magnesium can reduce stomach acid production, which will interfere with digestion.

TOXICITY LEVELS AND CAUSES OF DEFICIENCY

Magnesium toxicity (hypermagnesia) is rare but can occur when urinary excretion of magnesium is unusually decreased. Dr. Michael Colgan, however, cautions that magnesium can be toxic in amounts over ten grams, especially if taken over a long period of time.

Dr. Sheldon Hendler, M.D., Ph.D., cites two situations in which increasing magnesium intake is not desirable. He maintains that magnesium should not be administered to those suffering with severely decreased kidney function and in those with such heart problems as high-grade atrioventricular blocks or bifascicular blocks. According to Dr. Hendler, in these instances, magnesium could slow down the heart rate and lead to depression of neuromuscular function and even to respiratory depression.

Ironically, according to Dr. Hendler, many individuals suffering with these blocks may be suffering from marginal magnesium deficiency, in part because they often use diuretics and the heart drug digitalis. He cautions the safe use of over-the-counter magnesium-containing antacids and laxatives in these cases.

The amount of magnesium that is available for use by the body is diminished by excessive sugar intake, vomiting, diarrhea, excessive use of diuretics, and antibiotics. Excessive fat intake also reduces the amount of magnesium that can be absorbed by the small intestine. When intake of magnesium is low, the kidneys try to conserve levels of magnesium in the body by limiting its excretion.

Deficiency symptoms have been observed in people suffering from childhood malnutrition, intravenous feeding, malabsorption disorders, chronic alcoholism, kidney tubular dysfunction, genetic defects in gastrointestinal function, and hyperparathyroidism (hyperactive thyroid gland), and with the use of certain diuretics.

Phosphate-rich soft drinks can cause a magnesium deficiency due to its interference with absorption. Typical sodas contain about 30 milligrams of phosphate. For every milligram of phosphate contained in the beverage, one milligram of magnesium is destroyed in the body.

8 PHOSPHORUS

Phosphorus is found in every cell in the body and amounts to about two pounds in an average-sized person. Often called the metabolic twin of calcium, phosphorus is located in the bones and works as a partner with calcium to build strong bone. The same factors that control calcium absorption also determine the amount of phosphorus absorbed. These factors include vitamin D, the calcium-phosphorus ratio, and the amount of body need.

A healthy body will maintain a calcium-phosphorus balance in the bones of 2.5 parts calcium to 1 part phosphorus. An imbalance between phosphorus and calcium can result in increased calcium loss, which in turn can cause bone loss and osteoporosis to occur.

Human milk provides adequate phosphorus for the full-term infant, but additional phosphorus (which can be provided with additional feedings) has been shown to be required by premature infants in order to meet their more rapid growth needs.

ROLES IN THE BODY

In addition to its importance in the bones, phosphorus is also important to fat within the body. It combines with fat to form phospholipids. These are functional structures of all cell membranes and help transport nutrients through cell walls.

Phosphorus is a critical nutrient in the nucleus of the cell, forming part of the nucleic acids deoxyribonucleic (DNA) and ribonucleic (RNA) acid. Deoxyribonucleic acid carries the genetic material that has the encoding plans for the construction and function of each living organism. Scientists believe that damage of the DNA is the central feature in the onset of aging and cancer. Ribonucleic acid serves as the messenger for DNA. RNA delivers instructions to structures outside the cell nucleus called ribosomes, which carry out the instructions.

It is this transfer of information that is vital to maintaining a state of internal equilibrium. If the instructions never make it to the cell's energy-producing site, namely the mitochondria, malfunctions and incomplete messages can result. If the cells' lysosomes, proteins that assist in the metabolism of nutrients that feed the cells, are defective, they may release an excessive amount of enzymes at one time, thus interfering with a cells' function or in some cases destroying it. Phosphorus plays a key role in the construction and maintenance of this delicate but key process in the mitochondria of a cell.

Phosphorus is present in many enzyme systems and is important in the production and storage of energy produced by carbohydrate metabolism. This energy is released in muscular and nervous activity. Since phosphorus is a constituent of the high energy compound adenosine triphosphate (ATP), it is necessary for energy transductions essential for all cellular activity. Energy transduction is the transfer of energy from one system to another.

In the process of phosphorylation, ATP transfers one of its phosphate molecules to another substance, such as glucose (blood sugar). Biologists Starr and Taggart state that this phosphate transfer to another molecule increases the second molecule's store of energy, which enables it to enter specific reactions. Based on these findings, we can conclude that phosphorus plays a major role in the production of energy.

Phosphorus-containing compounds serve as buffers to control the acid-base balance of the body and assist in the utilization of vitamin B complex. Phosphorus also:

• Assists in brain functions.

• Helps vitamin utilization.

• Is involved in the overall human metabolism.

• Stimulates the regular contractions of the heart muscles.

• Is necessary for proper skeletal growth.

• Is essential for proper kidney function.

RECOMMENDED DOSAGE AND TOXICITY LEVELS

The National Research Council recommends a daily intake of 800 milligrams of phosphorus for men and women. For optimum health, adult men and women should take in 2,500 milligrams daily. I do not recommend, however, the taking of supplemental phosphorus, as it is so prevalent in all of our foods. Most Americans probably consume too much phosphorus in relation to calcium and may even need to cut back their phosphorus consumption. While there are no known toxic effects of phosphorus, high phosphorus intakes impair the absorption of calcium and cause increased amounts of calcium to be drawn from bones.

FOOD SOURCES

Meat, poultry, eggs, and yellow cheese are the best sources of phosphorus. Carbonated soft drinks also contain large amounts of phosphorus and should actually be avoided, as these high intakes of phosphorus will cause impaired calcium absorption.

SUPPLEMENTS

As stated previously, most people probably obtain more phosphorus than they need in their diets, so phosphorus supplementation is not necessary. If there is phosphorus in your multimineral supplement, however, be sure that the amount is in a 1 to 2 ratio with the amount of calcium in the supplement.

9 POTASSIUM

Potassium is the key cation (a positively charged ion) in intracellular fluid (it composes 98 percent of the fluid), and small amounts are also present in extracellular fluid. It works with sodium to maintain proper fluid and pH (acid-base) balance. Found in all cells, potassium has a direct effect on cell mass. Because of this, it influences muscle activity, particularly of the cardiac muscle. It is also important for proper transmission of nerve impulses.

ROLES IN THE BODY

There is evidence that indicates that potassium has a protective effect against chronic sodium chloride (table salt) toxicity. According to Dr. George R. Meneely, emeritus professor of medicine at Louisiana State University Medical Center, extensive animal and human studies show that the hypertensive effect of excessive sodium is counteracted with extra dietary potassium.

Although no one knows exactly how potassium protects the body from hypertension even when sodium intake isn't restricted, there are a number of theories. For one, potassium is an effective diuretic, and in addition to helping the body rid itself of water, potassium helps excrete extra sodium, an effect called *natriuresis*.

J. He and fellow researchers surmised from their research that the positive actions potassium has on hypertension is in part related to its effects on other nutrients. These researchers found that inadequate intake of potassium lowers urinary excretion of sodium, which allows sodium levels in the body to rise; while higher potassium intakes increase urinary sodium losses and reduce the harmful effects of sodium.

Moreover, scientists in Israel looked at the eating habits of ninety-eight vegetarians whose average age was sixty and compared them with a similar group of meat eaters. They found that the incidence of hypertension among the vegetarians was very low compared with the meat eaters. The vegetarians in this study ate as much salt as their counterparts and had the same predisposition to develop hypertension, but they didn't develop the condition. The researchers concluded that it was their potassium-rich diets of vegetables and fruits that kept them from developing hypertension.

Diabetic patients are often deficient in potassium, and as they age, levels may dwindle even further. Untreated diabetes, characterized by increased urinary flow with increased losses of potassium and sodium, may cause potassium in the bloodstream, where it is needed, to be forced into the cells. This condition, called hypokalemia, can have serious consequences. It could lead to growth impairment, brittle bones, paralysis, sterility, muscle weakness, central nervous system changes, renal hypertrophy, faulty heart rhythmic patterns, and death.

Potassium also:

- Curtails neuromuscular irritability.

- Acts as catalyst in carbohydrate and protein metabolism.

- Aids in the synthesis of glycogen and protein.

- Is necessary for normal muscle tone, nerves, and heart action.

- Is involved in the transfer of energy.

- Is an important nutrient for cellular respiration.

RECOMMENDED DOSAGE

There is no Recommended Dietary Allowance for potassium. It has been estimated that adults need 2,500 milligrams (2.5 grams) of potassium daily. I would say adults need closer to 4,500 milligrams of potassium daily. The average American diet contains two to four grams of potassium. For this reason, dietary deficiency is unlikely to occur in the average healthy person. However, when using supplemental potassium, never take it on an empty stomach. It can irritate your stomach and intestines.

FOOD SOURCES

Natural sources of potassium include leafy green vegetables, citrus fruits, and bananas.

SUPPLEMENTS

Potassium can be purchased in liquid, tablet, and capsule form, usually as potassium chloride and potassium gluconate.

TOXICITY LEVELS AND DEFICIENCY SYMPTOMS

With a daily intake of 25 grams of potassium chloride, symptoms of toxicity have been observed. Symptoms may include muscle fatigue, irregular heartbeat, and possibly heart failure.

A deficiency of potassium can occur as a result of such health disorders as diarrhea, vomiting, anorexia nervosa, or alcoholism; as a result of fasting; and with chronic use of diuretics and laxatives. During these periods, potassium levels should be monitored carefully.

Potassium loss may cause muscle weakness, cramps, loss of appetite, apathy, and listlessness. Either too little or too much potassium in the body can produce signs of heart disease on an electrocardiogram by interfering with the electrical conductivity of the heart muscle. A low level of potassium can impede or work against the actions of digitalis given for heart disease.

10   SODIUM

Although the American diet consists of far too much sodium, this mineral is important to many metabolic activities. As the chief cation (a positively charged ion) in extracellular fluid (fluid outside the cell), sodium acts with potassium, the principal cation in intracellular fluid (fluid inside the cell) to regulate and maintain body fluid balance. Sodium also helps to control cell permeability for easy exchange of substances across cell walls, and to activate the transmission of electrochemical impulses along the nerve membranes.

All dietary sodium is absorbed from the small intestine. Its metabolism is initiated by the adrenal cortex hormone aldosterone. This hormone controls sodium resorption from the kidneys, thus eliminating the possibility of overexcretion and sodium deficiency. However, sodium excretion is correlated to the levels of water in the body. Sodium is lost from the body as water is excreted, such as through urination, sweating, and defecation. When excessive amounts of water and sodium are lost, such as with diarrhea, vomiting, or profuse sweating, low blood volume, low blood pressure, and muscle cramping can result.

Sodium also:

- Functions with potassium to equalize the acid-alkali factor in the blood.

- Keeps other blood minerals soluble.

- Works with chlorine to improve blood lymph health.

- Helps purge carbon dioxide from the body.

- Aids in digestion.

- Is necessary for hydrochloric acid production in the stomach.

RECOMMENDED DOSAGES

Estimated safe and adequate daily intakes of sodium according to the National Academy of Sciences are 500 milligrams for men and most women, 569 milligrams for pregnant women, and 635 milligrams for lactating women. Keep your sodium intake around these amounts.

FOOD SOURCES

Common table salt is the main dietary source of sodium. Other natural food sources include milk, meat, eggs, and certain vegetables, such as carrots, beets, spinach, and other leafy greens.

SUPPLEMENTS

While sodium is essential to health, most Americans receive far too much in their diets, so I do not recommend supplementation.

TOXICITY LEVELS AND DEFICIENCY SYMPTOMS

An intake of 14 to 21 grams of salt daily is considered excessive and may cause symptoms of toxicity. Such symptoms include edema (swelling due to water retention) and elevated blood pressure. However, due to a woman's increased body mass during pregnancy, there may be an increased need for sodium during this time—up to 25 grams daily.

There is evidence that indicates that sodium deficiency retards growth in animals.

11   SULFUR

S ulfur is a nonmetallic element that occurs widely in nature. It makes up 0.25 percent of the human body's weight.

ROLES IN THE BODY

Dubbed nature's "beauty mineral," sulfur keeps the hair glossy and smooth and keeps the complexion clear and youthful. Contained in the amino acids methionine, cystine, and cysteine, sulfur appears to be necessary for collagen synthesis. Sulfur also combines with nitrogen, carbon, hydrogen, and oxygen to build protein, a main ingredient of muscles, skin, and organs.

Sulfur is a participant in many necessary reactions in the liver. It aids the liver in the secretion of bile, which helps break down and enhance the absorption of fats. In the liver, sulfur also latches on to toxic substances to help render them harmless, and it protects the red blood cells from destructive free radicals.

Collagen is made of protein and is the pre-eminent

structural molecule of the body, making up about 30 percent of the body's protein. In other words, it is the glue that holds us together. Collagen is vital for the growth and repair of body cells, gums, blood vessels, bones, and teeth. However, as we age, our bodies become less elastic, less agile, and more rigid. In turn, during the aging process, there is a progressive increase of cross-linking of many of the bodily constituents described above.

Cross-linking is an oxidative reaction in which undesirable bonds form between proteins, including the nucleic acids (RNA and DNA), or between lipids. As a result, the molecule cannot assume the correct shape for proper functioning.

Though some cross-linkage is required in order to maintain protein rigidity and structure, cross-linking can build up, causing considerable damage to life-giving metabolic processes. The process has been implicated as a cause of the onset of hardening of artery walls, a factor in atherosclerosis and hypertension. Cross-linking is also responsible for removing the elasticity from lung tissue, causing the disease known as emphysema, a very serious condition associated with smoking. Cross-linking is involved with the mechanisms responsible for the wrinkling of the skin and the loss of flexibility with age. It also takes part in the development of rigor mortis.

Many factors in our environment and some substances made by the body as part of normal metabolism can cause this cross-linking damage. Acetaldehyde (a chemical in cigarette smoke), alcohol, toxic products of faulty fat metabolism, smog, and other pollutants are all associated with unwanted cross-linkage.

Sulfur controls this unwanted cross-linking. A panel of researchers headed up by Dr. Herbert Sprince found that cysteine contains sulfur in a form that can inactivate potentially toxic substances such as aldehydes (toxic byproducts of the metabolism of alcohol). Further, Edes and associates reported that rats fed methionine- and cysteine-deficient diets have lower levels of certain enzymes that are protective against carcinogens (cancer-causing agents).

Early researchers Oeriu and Vacnitsu revealed significantly increased life spans of guinea pigs and mice injected with the sulfur-containing amino acid cysteine. Researcher Harmon also found substantial increases in life spans among cysteine-supplemented mice. Tas and coworkers have noted a decline in age-related influences with sulfur-containing substances. Weitzman and Stossel have claimed that cysteine may participate in some forms of DNA repair.

Sulfur also:

- Works with thiamine, pantothenic acid, and biotin.

- Plays a part in tissue respiration.

- Works with the liver to secrete bile.

- Helps maintain overall body balance.

RECOMMENDED DOSAGES

There is no Recommended Dietary Allowance for sulfur. This is because it is assumed that a person's sulfur requirement is met when protein intake is adequate. One would need to consume fifty to sixty grams of protein a day to maintain adequate levels of sulfur in the body. Those whose diets may be protein-deficient should take 300 milligrams of methyl-sulonyl-methane (MSM), one gram of cysteine with 3,000 milligrams of vitamin C, 50 milligrams of glutathione three times a day, or 19 milligrams of methionine per kilogram of body weight (To convert pounds into kilograms, divide weight in pounds by 2.2.) to maintain adequate levels of sulfur in the body. (See Supplements below.)

FOOD SOURCES

Meat, fish, and dairy products provide ample sulfur in the amino acids methionine, cysteine, cystine, and taurine. Eggs are also good sources. Onions and garlic are good sources for vegetarians. Vegetarians who do not eat eggs may become deficient in sulfur.

SUPPLEMENTS

Sulfur can be found in the amino-acid supplement cysteine; however, be sure to take three times as much vitamin C as cysteine when using this form. This will help prevent symptoms of toxicity. Sulfur can also be obtained through the amino-acid supplements glutathione and methionine.

Sulfur can also be taken in a compound called methyl-sulonyl-methane (MSM). Methyl-sulonyl-methane is a naturally occurring sulfur compound found in the tissues and fluids of all plants, animals, and humans. It is virtually nontoxic and poses none of the risks associated with the taking of cysteine. I recommend that you use this form if you need supplemental sulfur.

TOXICITY LEVELS

When taking sulfur in the form of cysteine, kidney or bladder stones may develop. Be sure to take vitamin C along with cysteine to help prevent it from converting into cystine, which can cause bladder and or kidney stones. Researchers recommend supplementing two to three time as much vitamin C as cysteine. There is also mounting evidence that cysteine may interfere with insulin sensitivity. For this reason, it is advisable that diabetics do not take cysteine unless directed by their physicians. Cysteine without vitamin C can also increase such monosodium glutamate (MSG) symptoms of toxicity as dizziness and incoherence.

12   CHROMIUM

Chromium is a trace mineral required by our bodies in very small amounts. It is, however, an essential mineral and performs a function without which we could not live. Chromium is a required cofactor for all of the actions of the hormone insulin. That is, without chromium, insulin cannot function properly in the body.

ROLES IN THE BODY

Insulin under normal circumstances directs food to where it is most needed—generally to muscle, liver, or fat cells. Under ideal circumstances, our tissues are very responsive or sensitive to insulin, and only small amounts of it are required to efficiently dispose of carbohydrates, fats, and protein. When the body tissues become insulin-resistant, the small amounts usually needed to do the job are not enough. To compensate, the body produces more insulin to try to overcome the resistance of the tissues. The classic example of this resistance is diabetes. Chromium helps insulin to perform its functions effectively, in order to help the body function effectively.

According to the United States Department of Agriculture (USDA), only one in ten Americans gets the minimum recommended amount of chromium (50 micrograms) eating typical American diets. Well-established studies by Anderson and Kozlovsky show that both exercise and high sugar consumption increase the body's need for this trace element. A shortage of chromium in the diet can contribute to serious problems in weight maintenance, energy, stamina, and muscle building.

Investigations by early pioneer in chromium research O.A. Levander have associated a decline in body chromium with age. Some thirty years ago, Dr. Jean Mayer, one of the first American nutritionists to speak at the opening session of the Senate Committee Hearing on Nutrition and Human Needs (1968), made the following statement about chromium in her book *Human Nutrition*: "Elucidation of the role of chromium in maintaining normal glucose metabolism and preventing atherosclerosis could be an important contribution to medicine and public health in the next decade."

In 1957, Dr. Walter Mertz, a former chief of biological chemistry at Walter Reed Army Institute of Research, discovered the glucose tolerance factor (GTF—another term for chromium, due to its effects on blood-sugar levels). Two years later, trivalent chromium (a form of chromium found in the body, which has the ability to combine with other substances in bodily chemical reactions) was identified as the active ingredient in GTF. Within the decade, GTF's function to stimulate the reaction of insulin was finally described by Mertz. Dr. Mertz was one of the first researchers to raise the the possibility of chromium deficiency as a possible cause of diabetes, after observing tests on experimental animals. Rats fed a chromium-poor diet showed severely impaired glucose metabolism and diabetes-like symptoms with raised blood cholesterol levels.

Current research has also confirmed the results of Dr. Mertz's early research with chromium, which showed that chromium can be used as a deterrent to diabetes onset and elevated cholesterol levels. The heart researcher Simonoff reported that GTF supplementation (4 milligrams of chromium a day) improves glucose tolerance and cholesterol levels. Based on his findings, he also concluded that chromium supplementation may help diminish the risk for atherosclerosis (hardening of the arteries).

According to Dr. Jeffrey A. Fisher, author of *The Chromium Program*, chromium exists in two chemical states: hexavalent chromium and trivalent chromium. He went on to say that "hexavalant, or industrial chromium, can be toxic, but trivalent, or nutritional chromium, has extremely low toxicity—probably about that of water."

Trivalent chromium forms the biologically active organic complex called glucose tolerance factor (GTF). Preformed highly available GTF is present in many foods and can be synthesized in the body from organic chromium salts.

Henry Schroeder, a prominent mineral researcher at Dartmouth Medical School, New Hampshire, found that the chromium content of the aorta was significantly lower in subjects who died of coronary occlusion (an obstruction of an artery from the heart) than those who died of an accident.

Over the last thirty years, researchers have continued to unlock the many health-giving benefits of chromium. On March 22, 1989, this little known trace element hit the forefront in an Associated Press wire story titled, "Chromium Viewed as a Medical Breakthrough." However, researchers had discovered that when a special chelating agent was administered with chromium, chromium's absorption increased dramatically. This chelating agent is known as a "picolinate." This type of chromium (pronounced chromium pik-O-lin-ate) has re-established chromium as an important and effective mineral and spawned new research into its role in human nutrition. Chelating agents, as we learned in Chapter 4, help increase absorption of minerals into the bloodstream.

Dr. Gary Evans, Professor of Chemistry at Bemidji State University in Minnesota, who discovered chromium picolinate, first presented evidence of its ability to reduce blood cholesterol levels and lower harmful low-density lipoprotein (LDL) and lipoprotein A levels (the bad components of cholesterol) at the American Society for Experimental Biology in New Orleans.

Clinical studies on the effectiveness of chromium picolinate were also done in 1988 at Mercury Hospital by Dr. Ray Press in San Diego, California on diabetic patients and patients with elevated cholesterol levels. Also, in two scientific studies conducted at Bemidji State University in Minnesota, students taking 200 micrograms of chromium picolinate (and exercising moderately) lost 22 percent of their body fat and increased their muscle mass by 44 percent. Several medical doctors now use chromium picolinate as part of therapy for diabetic patients.

In a recent independent study conducted at the Linus Pauling Institute of Science and Medicine, chromium bound with niacin (chromium polynicotinate) was discovered to be very effective in maintaining insulin and blood glucose levels when compared with results of other chromium bound supplements tested. Dr. Walter Mertz has now prompted an independent investigation into the relationship between chromium and niacin. Be sure to keep an eye out for new research concerning chromium polynicotinate's effectiveness as it unfolds in the future.

Chromium also:

- Helps the transport of protein.

- Stimulates the activity of enzymes involved in the metabolism of glucose.

- Works with RNA and its building action.

- Helps reduce cholesterol levels.

- Is useful in the prevention of atherosclerosis.

RECOMMENDED DOSAGE

I recommend that adults take about 800 micrograms of chromium daily, since modern diets offer only sparse amounts of chromium, and chromium is poorly absorbed and rapidly excreted when highly refined foods are consumed.

FOOD SOURCES

Brewer's yeast, liver, meat, shellfish, chicken, cheese, legumes, raw fruits and vegetables, whole grains, black pepper, corn oil, and molasses are known to be good sources of chromium. Dr. Passwater notes that drinking water supplies only small amounts of chromium and that the levels of chromium found in food sources depend on the amount of chromium in the soil in which the food was grown.

SUPPLEMENTS

Chromium can be purchased in liquid, tablet, and capsule form as chromium picolinate, GTF chromium, yeast-free GTF chromium, chromium chloride, and chromium polynicotinate. Research has shown that all forms of chromium positively affect glucose metabolism; however, I highly recommend the use of chromium picolinate because it has been shown to be the most efficient.

DEFICIENCY SYMPTOMS

American soils are sorely lacking in this vital trace nutrient, which makes the typical American diet chromium deficient. The average adult takes in about 52 micrograms a day through diet. But even this is poorly absorbed, making supplementation necessary. Dr. Richard Passwater, author of *GTF Chromium* believes that unrecognized chromium deficiencies may be among the most serious nutritional problems today. According to Dr. Passwater, the following menu contains only about 5 micrograms of chromium but, nevertheless, seems balanced and nutritious to the average American:

- Breakfast: Prune juice, farina, eggs, toast, and milk or coffee.

- Lunch: Clam chowder, tuna fish sandwich, white cake, and tea.

- Dinner: Creamed cod fish, mashed potatoes, peas, apricots, and white bread.

TOXICITY LEVELS

There is no known toxicity associated with the use of

chromium; however, diabetics must be very careful when using chromium. Since chromium increases the effectiveness of insulin, a diabetic's need for medication or injected insulin will probably decrease while taking it. It is very important that a physician monitor diabetic patients taking chromium closely because hypoglycemia may result from the use of chromium and medication. Diabetics should use chromium only under the close supervision of their physicians.

13 COBALT

Cobalt is an essential mineral that is a component of vitamin B_{12}, or cobalamin. In nutritional and pharmacological literature, the term vitamin B_{12} is inclusive of all cobalt-containing substances. Cobalt activates a number of enzymes in the body and is necessary for the normal formation of red blood cells, as well as other body cells. Discovered by Minot and Murphy in 1926 as a substance in liver that had beneficial effects in treating pernicious anemia, it was later named the "extrinsic factor," since it came from an outside source.

ROLES IN THE BODY

There is evidence that cobalt is vital to the nervous system to prevent demyelination (the destruction of the outer covering of nerves). Demyelination can cause faulty nerve transmission to occur. Many researchers believe that prolonged cobalt deficiencies will result in neurological disturbances, such as memory loss, mood changes, slowing of the memory process, and in severe cases, psychosis.

Cobalt, which is also beneficial in fighting pernicious anemia, not only is difficult to get in food, but also when taken orally, its absorption into the bloodstream is seriously impeded. For this reason, for the treatment of serious conditions, doctors will employ the use of vitamin B_{12} injections to hasten absorption.

In order for cobalt to be absorbed into the bloodstream, it must first combine with what is known as intrinsic factor in the stomach. Intrinsic factor is a protein produced by the stomach, which transports cobalt into the bloodstream. Without intrinsic factor, cobalt cannot be absorbed into the bloodstream and is excreted from the body unused.

Cobalt also:

- Is used to treat hepatitis because of its action in protein synthesis.

- Helps fight bronchial asthma.

- Is essential for healthy skin.

- Is responsible for building hemoglobin.

- Assists in the activation of many enzyme functions.

- Functions as a substitute for manganese in the activation of several enzymes.

RECOMMENDED DOSAGE

There is no Recommended Dietary Allowance for cobalt. Current data suggest that a daily intake of 5 to 8 micrograms is sufficient; however, due to cobalt's inability to be effectively absorbed from the gastrointestinal tract, I suggest a daily intake of 50 to 500 micrograms to ensure

Preventing Pernicious Anemia

Is there anything you can do to prevent pernicious anemia? Unfortunately, no. Since pernicious anemia is defined as the absence of the intrinsic factor and is genetically determined, it cannot be prevented. In other words, this is an inborn metabolic defect.

People with pernicious anemia are those who just don't have intrinsic factor in their digestive juices. They are unable to absorb any ingested vitamin B_{12} into their bloodstreams. No amount of supplementation can correct this situation. In fact, as explained by Dr. David Reuben, M.D., author of "Everything You Always Wanted to Know About Nutrition," this is a serious disease and if not treated can have grave consequences, including death.

If you experience signs of pernicious anemia, Dr. Reuben suggests you see your doctor. Early warning signs, including general weakness, fatigue, heart palpitations, paleness, or nerve damage, should not be overlooked. Your doctor can confirm the diagnosis and give you injections to clear up your symptoms. Although this problem will not go away if left untreated, it can be kept in remission with adequate medical treatment.

that enough is absorbed into the bloodstream for optimal health.

FOOD SOURCES

Liver, kidneys, and animal protein are excellent sources of cobalt. It also occurs in buckwheat, figs, milk, and many green vegetables.

SUPPLEMENTS

Cobalt can be found in supplement form as vitamin B_{12} (cyanocobalamin) in multivitamin formulas. It can be found in liquid, tablet, capsule, and sublingual forms (sublingual preparations are those formulated to be placed under the tongue and dissolved there for faster absorption). Due to cobalt's poor absorption rate, I recommend using the sublingual form.

TOXICITY LEVELS AND DEFICIENCY SYMPTOMS

There is evidence that high intakes of cobalt may result in an enlarged thyroid gland. The body has a high tolerance for cobalt, but toxicity has been known to occur in men who are heavy beer drinkers. Although it is not known why this only occurs in men, this can result in congestive heart failure.

Animal protein is almost the only source where cobalt occurs naturally in foods in sufficient amounts. Some strict vegetarians (eating no eggs, fish, poultry, dairy products, or meat) may have a low intake of vitamin B_{12} (and thus cobalt) and a high intake of folic acid. This combination can conceal a B_{12} deficiency. Such persons should be aware of this fact and consider B_{12} supplementation.

Cobalt deficiencies can cause a number of negative changes in the nervous system. Dr. Oded Abramsky, M.D., of the Neurology Department of Hadassah University in Jerusalem, noted the following functional disorders in his research with cobalt deficiencies:

- Soreness and weakness in legs and arms.

- Diminished reflex response and sensory perception.

- Difficulty in walking and speaking (stammering) and jerking of limbs.

Early warning signs may not be fully noted until permanent mental deterioration and paralysis occurs. If caught in time, these symptoms can be reversible.

In the case of pernicious anemia, your doctor may give you injections of vitamin B_{12}, up to 100 millionths of a gram per week in the beginning, and then the same microscopic dose every month for a total of 1,200 millionth of a gram per year. As expressed by Dr. Reuben, receiving all of these injections may seem like a nuisance, but it sure beats death.

14   COPPER

opper's use in human nutrition was first demonstrated by Hart and coworkers in 1928, after discovering its role as a cofactor for proper iron assimilation. These findings were later reaffirmed by Elvehjem in 1935 when he found copper to be instrumental in the production of the chromoprotein in red blood cells known as hemoglobin.

ROLES IN THE BODY

As an essential trace element in human nutrition, copper is vital to respiration. The protein hemoglobin carries most of the oxygen in the blood and needs copper as well as iron for its synthesis and function. Reports have suggested that copper may be of great value in preventing the lung damage associated with emphysema.

The best evidence available for copper's role in human nutrition comes from children who have Menke's disease, according to Dr. Joseph R. Prohaska, Associate Professor of Biochemistry at the University of Minnesota

School of Medicine in Duluth. Menke's disease is a genetic disease of abnormal copper metabolism, which causes severe deficiency. This disease is sometimes referred to as "kinky-hair syndrome" because affected infants have peculiar kinky white hair. It may also cause mental retardation, and affected children may die by two or three years of age. Dr. Prohaska postulates that these symptoms are thought to reflect deficiencies of copper enzymes. Copper supplementation does not improve this condition.

Copper and Rheumatoid Arthritis

Current data indicate that there are 40 million Americans suffering from the debilitating effects of arthritis. The Centers for Disease Control and Prevention reports that the number of Americans with arthritis by the year 2020 will have increased by more than 57 percent.

Arthritis results in inflammation and soreness of the joints. Research suggests that rheumatoid arthritis is related to the body's immune system. Either the body is unable to produce enough antibodies to prevent viruses from entering the joints, or antibodies that are produced are unable to differentiate between viruses and healthy cells, thereby destroying the healthy cells. Rheumatoid arthritis may also result from allergic reactions to certain foods.

Scientists now know that copper plays a key role in slowing down the degenerative effects of rheumatoid arthritis. Research by Dr. Joe M. McCord suggests that superoxide dismutase (SOD), an antioxidant enzyme made in the body, can prevent damage to the synovial fluid and membranes within the joints. SOD is the fifth most abundant protein in our bodies. One form of SOD contains copper and zinc, and another contains magnesium.

Previously, scientists believed that elevated copper levels in rheumatoid arthritis sufferers were responsible for the progression of the disease. Researchers now know that copper's presence is *in response* to the disease's onset. Current data indicate that copper in response to disease states and inflammatory disturbances interacts with ceruloplasmin (pigments in fats) to inhibit free-radical formation. Free radicals are highly reactive molecules implicated in over sixty age-related disorders.

Additional Benefits of Copper

Copper may be of benefit in protecting smooth muscle cells, collagen fibers, and especially elastin, the fibrous material that gives our skin its flexibility. For the elderly, copper plays an important role in the prevention of artherosclerosis. According to researchers Henning and Stuart, copper deficiencies can cause premature aging of arteries, which can lead to increased occurrence of atherosclerosis.

Copper also:

- Is involved in metabolism.

- May contribute to good immunity.

- Is beneficial for healthy heart action.

- Is an important component of protein associated with cellular oxidation.

- Works with vitamin C in the synthesis of collagen.

RECOMMENDED DOSAGE

Adult men and women need about 9 milligrams of copper per day for optimum health. Because copper is so widely available in the diet, most do not need to supplement with copper. Consult with a doctor or nutritionist if you suspect that you may be deficient in copper.

FOOD SOURCES

Copper is found in most foods, especially meats, whole-grain cereals, legumes, raisins, and drinking water.

SUPPLEMENTS

Copper is generally found in most multi-vitamin and -mineral supplements and as an individual supplement as copper oxide, copper gluconate, copper citrate, and copper sulfate, as well as protein chelates. I recommend the citrate or protein chelated forms of supplemental copper, although all forms are sufficient. If you take a multi-vitamin and -mineral supplement that contains copper, I recommend that you do not take any additional supplemental copper, unless specified by your health-care professional.

TOXICITY LEVELS AND DEFICIENCY SYMPTOMS

Dr. Herbert Scheinberg, Professor of Medicine at Albert Einstein College of Medicine in New York City, states that because our bodies have mechanisms to detoxify copper and get rid of it, it is hard to get copper poisoning. However, copper toxicity can occur. Excess doses of copper can cause a metallic taste in the mouth, hair loss, insomnia, nausea, vomiting, diarrhea, abdominal pains, headache, dizziness, irregular menses, and depression. Left untreated, this condition can be fatal. I do not recommend that anyone take supplemental copper in

amounts exceeding 2 milligrams per day unless specified by one's health-care practioner.

In Wilson's disease, a rare genetic disorder, copper
accumulates in the liver, causing toxicity to the body.
Symptoms include hepatitis, kidney disorders, and neurological disorders.

Symptoms of copper deficiency include fatigue, anemia and other blood disorders, decreased amounts of
calcium in the bones, small skin hemorrhages, and
aneurysms in the arteries.

15   FLUORINE

luorine is essential for maintenance of the bones and teeth. It is present in very small amounts in nearly every human tissue. Fluorine occurs in the body in compounds called fluorides.

ROLES IN THE BODY

Fluorine plays a major role in preventing osteoporosis. To assess effects of fluorine on osteoporosis, researchers at the University of Texas Southwestern Medical Center discovered that long-term fluoride and calcium supplementation can reduce fractures and increase bone mass.

In experiments, calcium citrate was given twice daily to 110 women with postmenopausal osteoporosis. Half of these women also received 25 milligrams of slow-release sodium fluoride, and half received a placebo (a substance having no medicinal value). Bone mass remained stable in the placebo group but increased in the group supplemented with fluoride. Also, 83 percent of the women using calcium and fluoride in this study remained fracture-free throughout the study, while only

65 percent of the women administered placebos were fracture-free.

RECOMMENDED DOSAGE AND TOXICITY LEVELS

Although traces of fluorine are beneficial to the body, excessive amounts are definitely harmful. Dr. Earl Mindell warns that most Americans have fluorine added to their water and do not need more than that. He also cautions that too much fluorine causes discolored teeth, and continued overuse, instead of strengthening bones, may cause them to fracture easily.

Fluorine is very dangerous in excess, especially in the form of sodium fluoride, which is the form added to our drinking water. Amounts of sodium fluoride in our drinking water exceeding two parts sodium fluoride per million parts water are considered dangerous. Health officials expressed concern with flourine overuse because studies have shown that it can destroy the enzyme phosphatase, which is important to many body functions, including the metabolism of vitamins. Fluorine also appears to be especially antagonistic toward brain tissue. Sodium fluoride can cause degenerative effects in the liver, adrenal glands, and reproductive organs. I warn against supplementing with fluorine in almost all circumstances, except on the advice of your physician.

SUPPLEMENTS

The taking of supplemental fluorine is not recommended. Supplemental fluorine is available, however, in prescription multi-vitamin and -mineral formulas for children in areas where water is not fluoridated.

FOOD SOURCES

Drinking water, tea, and seafood are sources of fluorine.

16   IODINE

odine is an essential micromineral that represents only about 0.0004 percent of body weight. In 1896, C. M. Baumann discovered that the thyroid gland was rich in this element, and as such, it was acknowledged as an essential micronutrient for animals and humans. Iodine is a component of the thyroid hormone thyroxin. When there is too little iodine, there is a deficiency of thyroxin. This can result in pathological changes in the thyroid gland and in the rest of the body.

ROLES IN THE BODY

Iodine is necessary and essential in human nutrition. It plays a major role in the development and function of the thyroid gland. Within the thyroid gland, it is a component of the hormones thyroxine and triiodothyronine. These hormones enter the cells of the surrounding tissues and bind to cellular substances, where they are thought to have a profound effect in controlling cellular metabolism.

Current interest in iodine has centered around radioactive fallout, which contains radioactive iodine. If the thyroid gland is deficient in iodine, the radioactive form will move into the thyroid, where it can cause thyroid cancer. After the accident at the nuclear power plant in Chernobyl, Ukraine, in 1986, potassium iodide was issued to the local residents to prevent this from occurring.

The late naturopathic researcher Dr. Paavo Airola maintained that when the accumulation of radioactive iodine is sufficiently large, absorption takes place mainly in the thyroid gland. According to Airola, when the diet is amply supplemented with easily absorbable organic iodine (such as kelp) radioactive iodine is not absorbed by the body.

Iodine also:

- Increases the motility of the gastrointestinal tract.

- Greatly increases the reactivity of the nervous system.

- Increases the heart's efficiency in utilizing oxygen.

RECOMMENDED DOSAGE

The National Research Council recommends that adults take in at least 150 micrograms of iodine per day. For optimum health, however, I recommend that adults take in 1,000 milligrams per day. It is estimated that the average American takes in about 600 micrograms of iodine daily.

FOOD SOURCES

Seafood, liver, eggs, kelp, dairy, and iodized salt are good sources of iodine.

SUPPLEMENTS

Kelp is a good source of iodine. It can be found in tablet, powder, and liquid form.

TOXICITY LEVELS

Iodine naturally occurs in food and water and is generally not toxic at amounts under 1,000 micrograms. However, iodine prepared as a drug or medicine must be carefully prescribed because an overdose can be serious. Sudden large doses of iodine administered to humans with normal thyroid function may impair the synthesis of thyroid hormones.

Large amounts of ingested iodine may increase thyroid secretions. This is known as hyperthyroidism. This disorder is characterized by increased heart rate, elevated blood pressure, excessive sweating, weight loss, and intolerance of heat. Typically, the affected person shows signs of nervous, agitated behavior and has problems sleeping.

DEFICIENCY SYMPTOMS

With iodine deficiency, the thyroid secretions are abnormally low. This condition is known as hypothyroidism. In adults, symptoms of lethargy, fatigue, a strong sensitivity to cold, and dried-out skin are common.

People who live in areas of the world where the food contains very little iodine cannot produce enough thyroxine. As a result, their metabolic rates decrease below normal, which stimulates the thyroid gland in an attempt to make increased quantities of thyroxine. This stimulus is, however, incapable of increasing the output of thyroxine when ample iodine is lacking. The end result is an enlargement of the thyroid gland. This enlargement is known as endemic goiter. Endemic goiter was formerly widely prevalent in the Great Lakes region of the United States and in the Swiss Alps, where little iodine is present in the soil. Researchers found that by giving people a little extra iodine in their table salt, goiter could be abolished.

Iodine deficiency in infants results in hypothyroidism, which results in a condition called cretinism. Cretinism is a devastating disorder characterized by constipation, poor appetite, jaundice, and slowed bone growth. Inadequate maternal iodine stores can result in impaired physical and mental development of the fetus. The basal metabolic rate is lower, the muscles are flabby, and the bones are poorly formed. If left untreated, severe and irreversible mental retardation will result.

17 IRON

ron is probably one of the most well-known minerals, as well as one of the most misunderstood. There are two different sources of iron in the human body. The main source is present in hemoglobin (the protein that carries oxygen in the red blood cells), myoglobin (a form of hemoglobin), and various oxidative enzyme systems. These sources of iron are known as functional sources. About one-fourth of the body's iron, is stored as iron-protein complexes (ferritin and hemosiderin) in the cells of bone marrow, liver, and spleen. Smaller quantities can be found in other cells. These stored forms serve as iron reserves. This iron pool can vary from 1,000 milligrams in a healthy male to 200 to 400 milligrams in women prior to menopause, but it is lower in iron-deficient individuals.

ROLES IN THE BODY

The major function of iron is to work with copper in the formation of hemoglobin. It is involved with the entire process of respiration to produce biological energy, without which life could not be sustained. Usually bound to protein, iron and its compounds serve as the carriers of life-giving oxygen to cells.

To regulate the respirative actions of iron, the body has a built-in conversion or recycling process that maintains adequate levels. There is no effective way to regulate the excretion of iron; however, its absorption can be regulated. When the body's iron is at acceptable levels, the intestinal mucous protective lining will increase or decrease iron absorption, depending on the amounts in the body, to maintain the necessary levels. When the iron levels become low, absorption increases. According to Dr. Eric Trimmer, a noted trace element researcher, the body normally absorbs about 6 to 10 percent of iron from food, but an iron-deficient person can absorb up to 60 percent. Dr. Trimmer maintains that this mechanism is not fully understood as of yet.

Although the body has a built-in mechanism to protect itself from iron overload, this regulatory mechanism is not perfect, and the body could absorb more than is needed. This could result in a malady called hemochromatosis. Severe damage to the liver, heart, and pancreas could occur. This iron overload can also increase susceptibility to bacterial infections because these organisms need extra iron to grow and it is then made available.

Balance is the key. Keep your iron intake within the range of the RDAs (see page 117), or see a doctor before you decide to take supplemental iron.

Iron also:

- Helps fight fatigue.

- Wards off infection.

- Enhances the function of lymphocytes.

- Helps promote antibodies.

- Works to improve functions of neurotransmitting chemicals.

- Is involved with the production of carnitine (the amino acid responsible for fatty acid synthesis).

- Is instrumental in the production of collagen and elastin (components of connective tissue).

- Protects against oxidative damage.

- Produces and regulates several brain neurotransmitters.

High intakes of phosphorus, cellulose (plant fibers), coffee, and tea can interfere with iron absorption. Vitamin C enhances the body's ability to utilize iron properly.

RECOMMENDED DOSAGES

The Recommended Dietary Allowance for iron is 18 milligrams for most women and 10 milligrams for men. Women need more iron than men, as the need for iron increases during menstruation. While the Recommended Dietary Allowance is sufficient for men, I recommend that women take more than the Recommended Dietary Allowance. Most women should take from 18 to 35 milligrams per day. Pregnant and lactating women need 30 to 60 milligrams of iron per day, and postmenopausal women need about 10 milligrams per day as iron needs decrease after menopause. Adult men who eat well-balanced diets of 2,000 calories or more do not need iron supplementation. In fact, some researchers believe that the higher incidence of coronary heart disease in men, as compared with women, in more affluent cultures is possibly due to higher levels of stored iron in men.

FOOD SOURCES

Liver and sunflower seeds are excellent sources of iron. Dark green leafy vegetables, bananas, dark grapes, black-strap molasses, black beans, sesame seeds, and egg yolks are also good sources of iron.

SUPPLEMENTS

Iron can be purchased as an individual supplement or as part of multimineral formulas; as tablets, liquids, or capsules; in timed-release form; and as iron gluconate, iron sulfate, iron oxide fumarate, iron glycinate, iron citrate, or iron chelated to a protein, among others.

The most used iron supplement is iron sulfate. I recommend taking iron citrate, iron gluconate, or iron fumarate, as these forms are less irritating to the stomach than the other forms and less likely to cause constipation, as many iron supplements may. I do not recommend taking timed-release iron supplements, as these may cause an iron overload in the blood, which has been associated with heart disease.

DEFICIENCY SYMPTOMS

Your diet must contain more iron than your body actually needs, since only a small percentage of iron taken in is actually absorbed into the bloodstream; however, you must watch your intake carefully to prevent possible iron overload. Typical American diets, high in fats, sugars, and calories, with little or no nutrient base, provide small amounts of needed iron—about 6 milligrams per 1,000 calories.

Those groups at risk for iron deficiencies are infants; adolescents; premenopausal women, especially those on low-calorie diets; pregnant and lactating women; vegetarians; and the elderly. These deficiencies can cause several adverse effects. An inability to exercise and muscle weakness are common symptoms of iron deficiencies. Infants who are iron-deficient are often irritable and lack interest in their surroundings. In experimental research, iron deficiency has been found to hasten chemical tumor induction in rats.

Anemia is a disorder in which the number of red blood cells or the amount of hemoglobin in them is low. It is characterized by fatigue and shortness of breath. Research has confirmed that adequate levels of iron are necessary to prevent iron-deficient anemia. Anemia occurs when the red blood cell count falls below about 15 trillion. A normal red blood cell count would be about 25 trillion. It is not advisable, however, to self-treat or diagnose this condition, since all anemias are not necessarily caused by an iron deficiency. Other factors associated with the onset of anemia are chronic internal bleeding; long-term deficiencies of folic acid, vitamin B_6, or copper; and impaired absorption (as with alcoholism or constant intestinal impairments).

Past and present investigations have revealed that women, due to menstrual cycles, are more prone to developing iron-deficiency anemia. In an early ground-breaking study into menstruation's effect on iron stores, Hallberg and associates in Goteborg, Sweden, studied menstrual blood loss in a randomly selected sample of 476 women.

The relationship of menstrual blood loss and iron-deficiency anemia was clearly demonstrated by the fact that subjects whose menstrual blood losses exceeded 60 milliliters showed a statistically significant decrease in hemoglobin concentration and plasma iron. They also showed a marked decrease in iron-binding capacity (iron must be bound to a protein in the blood to be used by the body) and no stored iron in the bone marrow.

TOXICITY LEVELS

Symptoms of toxicity may occur with amounts of iron exceeding 75 milligrams per day. Such symptoms may include constipation, diarrhea, and/or nausea. Iron toxicity in children can have severe consequences. In a dangerous condition called hemochromatosis, too much iron is absorbed into the bloodstream, leading to a buildup of iron in the tissues of the organs. This can result in damage to the organs, and possibly death if left untreated. However, once identified, this condition is treatable.

18   MANGANESE

anganese was first recognized in 1931 by the researchers Orent and McCollum.

ROLES IN THE BODY

Investigations have demonstrated the role of manganese in bone structure, reproduction, and nervous system activity. Manganese also acts as a partner to choline in fat metabolism.

Manganese and Bone Structure

In a study of women with osteoporosis, manganese was found to be very beneficial in slowing the disease's progression. Manganese (along with copper and fluoride) is involved with hardening of the bones.

Some recent developments about the effects of manganese on good bone health were uncovered by doctors working with Hall of Fame basketball star Bill Walton.

Walton was constantly plagued by broken bones, and doctors and trainers worked to correct this problem. Tests showed that Bill had plenty of calcium in his bones, but he still suffered from bone breakage and joint pain. Later it was revealed that he had extremely low levels of manganese. After six weeks of supplementation with this trace mineral, his bone strength had increased, and he was able to resume his career. The rest is history.

Manganese and Rheumatoid Arthritis

Dr. George C. Cotzia, who developed the use of levodopa in the treatment of Parkinson's disease, reported at the First Annual Conference on Trace Substances in Environmental Health at the University of Missouri in 1967 that manganese was necessary for the enzymatic synthesis of a material called mucopolysaccharide, which is deficient in those with rheumatoid arthritis.

Mucopolysaccharides help form major cushioning components of the joint fluids and surrounding tissue. It helps make the synovial joint fluid thick and elastic. Tissues in the joints can become damaged when the lubricating synovial fluids in the joint spaces become thin and watery. The normal cushioning is lost, which causes the bone and cartilage to scrape against one another. This causes cartilage to erode, producing pain and problems with movement and flexibility. Current research has confirmed that adequate levels of manganese are essential to the utilization of mucopolysaccharides.

In early investigations, researchers had theorized that if manganese was involved with the synthesis of mucopolysaccharides, it would repair worn-out cartilage. Researchers Quillen (author of *Healing Nutrients*) and Hendler (author of *The Complete Guide to Anti-Aging*

Nutrients) suggested that, although research into this phenomenon is anecdotal, it did warrant further review.

Manganese and Nerve Transmission

There is increasing evidence that manganese may have some benefit in the treatment of neurological disorders. Multiple sclerosis, a disorder characterized by a breakdown of the myelin sheath that protects the nerves, has been treated with manganese. A lack of manganese is one factor in this disorder. It also appears that a lack of this mineral may be a factor in the cause of myasthenia gravis, an autoimmune neuromuscular disorder affecting muscle strength. Studies also indicate that low manganese levels are connected with schizophrenia and certain seizures.

Manganese and Reproduction

There is evidence that manganese may play a vital role in the reproductive process. In animal studies, researchers have found that a manganese deficiency causes atrophy of the reproductive organs. Manganese is also involved in the synthesis of cholesterol in the body. Cholesterol is necessary for the production of sex steroids, so a manganese deficiency may interfere with this process.

Additional Benefits of Manganese

Manganese contributes to the activation of the immune system's defensive response to abnormal cell growth by interacting with the antioxidant enzyme superoxide dismutase (SOD). Many tumors have been found to contain considerably lower than normal levels of SOD containing manganese.

In fact, during a four-month study of forty-seven women, Drs. Cindy Davis and J. L. Greger of the Department of Nutritional Sciences at the University of Wisconsin in Madison discovered that poor manganese intake actually lowered the activity of SOD in white blood cells. Manganese supplementation resulted in considerable increases of "manganese-dependent SOD activity" in white blood cells as reported in the *American Journal of Clinical Nutrition.*

Manganese also:

- Helps nourish the nerves and brain.

- Is essential for the formation of the hormone thyroxin.

- Is important for the production of breastmilk.

- Plays a part in protein, carbohydrate, and fat metabolism.

- Helps maintain sex hormones.

RECOMMENDED DOSAGE

Manganese is far harder than other trace elements for the body to absorb, which makes keeping the manganese balance correct difficult. However, very little is needed. A daily intake of 10 milligrams of manganese daily should allow enough manganese to be absorbed into the bloodstream.

FOOD SOURCES

Egg yolks, sunflower seeds, wheat germ, whole-grain cereals and flour, dried peas, beans, and bone meal are good sources of manganese. Manganese also occurs in high concentrations in nuts and leafy vegetables.

SUPPLEMENTS

Manganese can be found in multi-vitamin and -mineral formulas and as individual supplements. It is usually in tablet form. It can be found as manganese gluconate, manganese sulfate, and manganese citrate. All of these forms are well absorbed, though manganese gluconate is less irritating to the digestive tract.

TOXICITY LEVELS

Manganese toxicity is not likely when the mineral is ingested. Very high dosages of manganese can result in reduced storage and utilization of iron and vice versa. Manganese toxicity can occur when the mineral is inhaled. C. C. Cotzias first reported manganese toxicity in miners who had inhaled dust ore. Research has further substantiated Cotzias' finding. Industrial workers frequently exposed to manganese dust may absorb enough of the metal in the respiratory tract to develop toxic symptoms. Symptoms of manganese toxicity may include speech impairment, leg cramps, delusions, depression, and increased sleeping.

DEFICIENCY SYMPTOMS

A lack of manganese has been related to schizophrenia, epilepsy, and various metabolic diseases. Research has shown that many schizophrenics have high copper levels. Manganese, like zinc, is effective in increasing copper excretion from the body. A deficiency of manganese has also been linked with pancreatic disturbances and diabetes.

19 MOLYBDENUM

Molybdenum is probably the least commonly known mineral but is best known for its role in eradicating the esophageal cancer that had been prevalent in the Lin Xian region of China for nearly 2,000 years. After the soil was fortified with this trace element and vitamin C was provided to the population, there has been a large drop in cancer rates. These nutrients appear to decrease the amount of nitrosamines (cancer-causing agents) and their precursors in the body. Low levels of molybdenum in the soil and a high rate of esophageal cancer in the Bantu of Transkei in South Africa have also been noted.

ROLES IN THE BODY

Adequate molybdenum levels are necessary for the proper formation of bone and teeth. It is also vital to fetal development and plays a major role in the formation of proteins.

Molybdenum also:

- Is important to copper and sulfur metabolism.

- Is an essential part of the enzymes xanthine oxidase (responsible for mobilizing iron from the liver) and aldehyde oxidase (necessary for the oxidation of fats).

- Is involved with proper carbohydrate metabolism.

- Plays a part in the prevention of anemia.

RECOMMENDED DOSAGE

No Recommended Dietary Allowance for molybdenum currently exists. The estimated safe and adequate intake is 0.15 to 0.5 milligrams daily. Stick to the recommended intake.

FOOD SOURCES

Animal organs, shellfish, vegetables, grains, fruits, and sunflower seeds are good sources of molybdenum. Brewer's yeast, brown rice, and naturally hard water also supply the body with molybdenum.

SUPPLEMENTS

Molybdenum can be found in many multi-vitamin and -mineral formulas.

TOXICITY LEVELS

Intakes of molybdenum exceeding 5 milligrams can be toxic. Such minerals as sulfur and copper compete with molybdenum for absorption at absorption sites, so they may reduce toxicity of molybdenum. Growth retardation and weight loss have consistently been reported in animals due to molybdenum toxicity. Molybdenum is a constituent of an enzyme necessary for the last stage of the metabolism of purines (large nitrogen compounds) into uric acid. Uric acid is a by-product of protein metabolism. Excessive uric acid can be deposited as crystals in the joints and kidneys in the painful and damaging disorder known as gout. High intakes of molybdenum can cause excessive uric-acid formation. There appear to be no deficiency symptoms for molybdenum.

20   SELENIUM

The eminent nutritional researchers Abram Hoffer and Morton Walker commented that in just over twenty years, selenium has changed from being classified as highly toxic to being classified as one of the essential trace elements. Dr. Klaus Schwarz and C. M. Katz had established that selenium was essential to life in 1957, but it was not until 1990 that the National Research Council determined a Recommended Dietary Allowance (RDA) for the mineral.

The distribution of selenium in the soil varies greatly throughout the world, including throughout the United States. Dr. Richard Passwater, Director of Research at Solgar Nutrition Research Center in Berlin, Maryland, and author of *Selenium as Food and Medicine*, contends that the original selenium content of soil is only part of the problem. While levels of selenium in soil are already low, they are being further eroded by modern fertilization. Artificial fertilizers upset the pH of the soil, which kills off beneficial bacteria in the soil. When this happens, any minerals that may be present in the soil cannot be properly absorbed by plants.

ROLES IN THE BODY

Like vitamin E, selenium has the capability of functioning as an antioxidant. Studies have also indicated that selenium may play a role in red blood cell formation.

Vitamin E and selenium work together in a potent anticancer, anti-aging enzyme called glutathione peroxidase. Glutathione peroxidase is like a miniature police force that wipes out renegade cells and free radicals within. Vitamin E is the only fat-soluble antioxidant in blood plasma, and the levels of glutathione peroxidase in the body depend greatly on the levels of vitamin E and selenium in the diet.

Selenium is present in all tissue and is highly concentrated in the kidneys, liver, pancreas, spleen, and testes. Male sperm cells contain high concentrations of selenium, which are lost during intercourse. For this reason, requirements may be higher for men.

Selenium deficiency has also been suggested as a possible factor in the cause of cancer. Trace amounts have been reported to be protective against human cancer in early studies.

Evidence that selenium helps prevent cancer is promising according to Patricia Hausman, author of *Foods That Fight Cancer*. Research has shown that blood selenium levels are higher in healthy people than in cancer victims, that selenium added to the diet or drinking water of laboratory animals helps to protect against cancer-causing chemicals, and that areas of the world where selenium intake is high have lower cancer rates than countries where the diet is low in selenium.

Researchers have found that many cancer patients

have below-normal selenium levels in their blood. Yet, according to Dr. Patrick Quillen, Ph.D., R.D., and author of *Healing Nutrients*, these findings are being disputed because many scientists believe that cancer precipitates the lower levels, meaning that cancer probably caused the low levels of selenium in the body, rather than the low selenium levels causing cancer. To confirm this hypothesis, nearly fifty studies of the anticancer effects of selenium were conducted by researchers at Cornell University. Blood samples were drawn from 10,000 Americans at the start of this study and then frozen. Over the next five years, blood samples of those who developed cancer were thawed and checked for selenium levels. Cancer victims were found to have the lowest levels of selenium in their blood at the start of the study. Low selenium levels in the blood actually doubled the risk of cancer.

In the late 1960s and early 1970s, Dr. Richard A. Passwater began experiments with selenium to find out if there was any correlation with its use and a decreased incidence of cancer, and thus an extended life span. Dr. Passwater chose selenium because it is a compound that might work with other compounds previously shown to extend life span, such as vitamin E and sulfur-containing amino acids. By 1969, he had successfully developed a range of combinations of antioxidant compounds that extended the average life span by 20 to 30 percent and the maximum life span by 5 to 10 percent in mice.

By 1971, Dr. Passwater's investigations had revealed that when aging accelerants were given to mice, selenium and its cofactors produced life-span increases of 175 percent compared with controls. Dr. Passwater had theorized that since studies show that there is some relationship between cancer and aging, if we can slow down the aging process, we will be less vulnerable to cancer and most other diseases. As a result of this and other studies, a great deal more is known concerning selenium's ability to help us live longer and better.

Experts have mapped the selenium levels in soil across the United States, then compared the cancer death rates of these cities. They found that the lower the selenium levels in the soil (and thus in the food supply), the higher the cancer incidence of people in that city.

Table 20.1 shows a clear correlation of cancer death rates and the selenium concentration in human blood. Note that in Rapid City, South Dakota, which has the highest blood levels of selenium of any municipality, the cancer death rate is the lowest in the country. According to Dr. Earl Mindell, this may be more than just a coincidence.

Rheumatologist Dr. U. Tarp and his colleagues carrying out research at the Rheumatism Research Unit at Achus in Denmark demonstrated that low activity of the selenium-dependent enzyme glutathione peroxidase may cause high levels of peroxidation products in rheumatoid arthritis. High levels of peroxidation products have been implicated as a major factor in the cause of rheumatoid arthritis.

Dr. Henry A. Schroeder of the Trace Mineral Laboratory of Dartmouth Medical School found selenium to be 100 times more effective in removing cadmium from the body in his research. Cadmium is a highly toxic mineral that the body utilizes when zinc is not present in adequate amounts. Dr. W. G. Hoekstra and his associates at the University of Wisconsin found mercury contents in tuna were less dangerous than previously suspected due to the presence of selenium. They found that selenium, which also concentrates in tuna, reduces the toxicity of ingested mercury.

N. W. Schoene and coworkers demonstrated that

Table 20.1. Selenium Concentrations in Blood and Cancer Death Rates in Various Cities

City	Blood Selenium Levels (mcg/100 ml)	Cancer Deaths Per 100,000
Rapid City, SD	25.6	94.0
Cheyenne, WY	23.4	104.0
Spokane, WA	23.0	179.0
Fargo, ND	21.7	142.0
Little Rock, AR	20.1	176.0
Phoenix, AZ	19.7	126.7
Meridian, MS	19.5	125.0
Missoula, MT	19.4	174.0
El Paso, TX	19.2	119.0
Jacksonville, FL	18.8	199.0
Red Bluff, CA	18.2	172.0
Geneva, NY	18.2	172.0
Billings, MT	18.0	138.0
Montpelier, VT	18.0	164.0
Lubbock, TX	17.8	115.0
Lafayette, LA	17.6	145.0
Canandaigua, NY	17.6	168.0
Muncie, IN	15.8	169.0
Lima, OH	15.7	188.0

platelets (the blood cells responsible for clotting) from selenium-deficient rats aggregated to form clots in the bloodstream more than those from selenium-supplemented rats did, increasing the risk of blood-clot formation, thus affecting proper blood flow to the heart. This could cause a heart attack to occur.

Selenium also:

- Is essential for reproduction.

- Preserves tissue elasticity.

- Is important for good heart health.

- Is a natural antioxidant.

- Helps the body increase the activity of vitamin E.

- Is responsible for the retention of vitamin E in the body.

- Prevents chromosome breaks.

RECOMMENDED DOSAGE

Take 200 micrograms of selenium daily.

FOOD SOURCES

The best food sources of selenium are brewer's yeast, garlic, liver, and eggs. Animal sources are much richer in selenium than are plant foods—if the animals ate a diet high in selenium. Processing of food greatly decreases its selenium contents.

SUPPLEMENTS

Selenium can be found in multi-vitamin and -mineral formulas and as individual supplements. It is usually in the form of selenium yeast, selenomethionine, selenate, and yeast-free protein chelates. Current data indicate that selenomethionine is better absorbed and poses less risk of toxicity, so I recommend this form. Those who are sensitive to yeast should take the yeast-free protein chelate form, as selenomethionine is extracted from yeast.

TOXICITY LEVELS

Severe overdose of selenium is very dangerous. Stick to the guidelines outlined by the National Research Council. According to the Food and Nutrition Board of the National Research Council, a long-term intake of 2,400 to 3,000 micrograms of selenium daily would be expected to cause a toxic reaction; however, it is unlikely that one could ingest these toxic levels of selenium strictly from food. Severe overdose produces fever and increased respiratory rate, gastrointestinal distress, and sometimes death. When it is consumed or inhaled at levels as high as 1,700 micrograms, selenium interferes with some important reactions in the body involving sulfur.

DEFICIENCY SYMPTOMS

Deficiencies of selenium can result in premature aging, nerve disorders, diminished vision, and can possibly cause infertility. Scientists are also researching the possibilities of selenium deficiencies leading to cancer and cardiovascular disease.

21   ZINC

The function of zinc as an important element in biochemistry was realized as early as 1869, when Raulin showed that it was necessary for the growth of molds. It was found in human liver around 1877, but it was not until 1934 that Gabriel Bertrand Paris showed that this metal was essential for the growth of the mouse. In 1935, Stirn, Elvejehm, and Hart proved that zinc was necessary for growth in rats. In 1974, zinc was accepted as essential, and a Recommended Dietary Allowance (RDA) was determined for it.

ROLES IN THE BODY

Data have indicated over the years that zinc is absolutely necessary for growth to occur in humans and that it increases resistance to disease. To date, researchers have found more than ninety zinc-dependent enzymes in the body, which is more than all of the other mineral-dependent enzymes combined. For this reason, zinc is sometimes referred to as "the whole-body mineral" or the "master mineral."

Trace amounts of zinc are present in all living matter. About 263 milligrams are distributed throughout the human body. Zinc is involved in most major metabolic reactions and in nucleic acid, carbohydrate, and protein metabolism. It is essential for growth and normal sexual development in children.

Dr. Earl Mindell, the well-known vitamin and mineral researcher, stated that zinc should be thought of as a traffic policeman, directing and overseeing the efficient flow of body processes, the maintenance of enzyme systems, and the integrity of our cells. Although only small amounts are found in our bodies, zinc is, nevertheless, a powerful catalyst that is absolutely necessary for most body functions. For example, zinc and chromium are necessary for the passage of glucose (blood sugar) from the blood into many body cells. The energy contained in glucose cannot be released until this passage is accomplished.

Dr. Eberhard Kronhausen and associates, authors of *Formula for Life: The Antioxidant, Free-Radical Detoxification Program,* refer to zinc as vitamin E's neglected twin brother. These researchers argue that while much of zinc is taken out of grains by our modern processing methods, cadmium, a very toxic metal, is present in the grain due to pollution in the soil, becomes concentrated in the inner white part of the grain, and will remain in refined flour. Zinc neutralizes this highly toxic metal because of its powerful antioxidant properties.

Dr. Sheldon Hendler points out that we accumulate an average of 30 milligrams of cadmium in our bodies, mainly in the kidneys. He maintains that we need to keep our zinc/cadmium ratio in favor of zinc as much as possible, since zinc is protective and cadmium is anything but. Cadmium can, for instance, produce sperm abnormalities and infertility.

Zinc is also involved with the production of DNA and RNA (our genetic blueprints). For this reason, a zinc deficiency can lead to dwarfism. Additionally, more than 100 enzyme systems, including the pancreatic system, depend on zinc for their proper functioning.

Zinc and vitamin A work together. When zinc is added to the diet, more vitamin A is needed. Dr. Michael Bunk, a research scientist at Memorial Sloan-Kettering Cancer Center in New York City, found that mice who were made deficient in zinc also became deficient in vitamin A. According to Dr. Bunk, it is well known that a zinc deficiency affects the release of stored vitamin A from the liver, but a second connection may be here. He thinks that a zinc deficiency impairs the uptake of vitamin A by the epithelial cells, putting them at risk for developing cancer or other diseases. The epithelial cells cover a surface, like the skin, or line a cavity, like the bladder. They are dependent on both vitamin A and zinc. The epithelial cells are also found in the mammary glands in the breasts.

Zinc and Cardiovascular Disease

Several studies have confirmed zinc's ability to protect cell walls, thus limiting the damaging effects associated with hardening of the arteries, known as atherosclerosis. W. J. Bettger and B. L. O'Dell propose that the action of zinc on cell membranes is both structural and functional. Since zinc is necessary for wound healing to occur, and atherosclerosis is thought to begin with a vessel-wall injury or dysfunction, researchers believe that low zinc concentrations could be the cause of both initiation of injury and inadequate tissue repair in atherosclerosis.

Researchers at the University of Kentucky found that when cells from the lining of the arteries were exposed to varying levels of zinc, their ability to resist invasion by harmful cholesterol was improved only when zinc levels were high. The results of this study proved that zinc deficiency damages the artery wall's ability to act as a barrier against the damage of fat peroxidation, while exposure to optimal levels of zinc strengthens the arteries against free-radical damage.

Zinc and Immunity

Low blood levels of zinc have been observed in AIDS (acquired immunodeficiency syndrome) patients. In fact, the lower the zinc levels are, the worse the disease and lower the level of immune function. In light of these recent findings, some researchers recommend zinc supplementation in addition to conventional therapy for AIDS patients.

Italian scientists believe that low levels of zinc, and not a faulty thymus gland, are directly responsible for immune suppression in the elderly and in children with Down's syndrome. The thymus gland produces a hormone called FTS. It has been found that the thymus glands of the elderly and those with Down's syndrome produce low levels of FTS. It was thought that these low levels of FTS were responsible for the high incidence of immune suppression in these two groups. However, it has been found that blood levels of zinc are also low among the elderly and those with Down's syndrome. So, it is quite likely that this could be the cause of the prevalent immune suppression in these two groups.

In another recent study, zinc supplementation (in the amount of 220 milligrams of zinc sulfate twice a day for one month) increased the number of T-lymphocytes circulating in the blood. T-lymphocytes help fight infection and improve antibody response.

Zinc and Testosterone

Dr. Isadore Rosenfeld, M.D., a clinical professor of medicine at New York Hospital/Cornell Medical Center, mentions that men have been eating oysters for years in attempts to increase their virility. Many do not know why oysters seem to have an effect on their sexual potence. The reason is that oysters are among the best sources of zinc. Current data clearly shows that there is a direct connection between the production levels of testosterone (the male sex hormone) and the amount of zinc in the body. Some research on the connection between the use of diuretics for hypertension and impotency suggests that zinc depletion from the use of the diuretics may be the cause of impotency rather than the drugs themselves.

Zinc and Growth and Development

Studies show that zinc is vital to the maturation process. As children reach adolescence, their normal serum zinc levels increase. Low levels of zinc retard the body's ability to utilize protein for growth, as shown in children with retarded growth.

Lowell E. Sever, Ph.D., formerly of the University of Washington School of Public Health in Seattle, was one of the first investigators to identify the connection between low levels of zinc and malformation, especially in the Near East countries, such as Egypt, Iran, and Turkey. Birth abnormalities associated with a lack of zinc during pregnancy have been found in Denver and Baltimore. Current data indicate that zinc levels influence cell division during pregnancy. When zinc levels are optimal, cell division occurs normally. When zinc stores drop below adequate levels, cell division has been shown to slow down or become more error prone.

Zinc also:

- Promotes wound healing.
- Fights infection by improving the function of white blood cells.
- Is helpful in cases of cystic fibrosis and Wilson's disease.
- Neutralizes copper.
- Is beneficial in treating anorexia nervosa.
- Is useful in treating rheumatoid arthritis.
- Is important for keratin production for healthy hair, skin, and nails.
- Is essential to stimulate taste and smell.
- Promotes healthy teeth and gums.
- Is important to the function of the thymus gland and immunity.

RECOMMENDED DOSAGE

While optimal intakes of zinc enhance immunity and further healthy desirable cell growth, too much zinc can actually *compromise* immunity, which can open the door for such degenerative diseases as atherosclerosis and cancer. Take 50 milligrams of zinc daily for optimum health.

TOXICITY LEVELS

High dosages of zinc may decrease copper levels in the

blood, which may actually be a positive effect for those with high blood levels of copper. Symptoms of toxicity include nausea, vomiting, and diarrhea. These symptoms can occur in those taking more than 150 milligrams per day for an extended period of time.

FOOD SOURCES

Raw oysters, chicken, pumpkin seeds, beef liver, Swiss cheese, dry roasted cashews, and the dark meat of turkey are excellent sources of zinc.

SUPPLEMENTS

Zinc supplements can be found as zinc sulfate, zinc gluconate, zinc citrate, zinc picolinate, zinc orotate, zinc oxide, or zinc chelated to a protein. These forms can be purchased as individual supplements or as part of a multimineral formula. Zinc comes in tablets, capsules, and liquid zinc picolinate. There is much research being conducted to determine the effectiveness of minerals other than chromium in the picolinate form; however, at this time, this research is inconclusive. I recommend taking zinc in the gluconate, citrate, or protein chelate forms.

DEFICIENCY SYMPTOMS

Zinc can drop to low levels in smokers, impairing the immune system as well as the ability to detoxify the poisons being absorbed. Low zinc levels lead to a greater uptake and absorption of the trace element cadmium, which is one of the toxins in tobacco smoke. Pregnant women who smoke are more likely to give birth to zinc-deficient babies. Nonsmokers who inhale unfiltered secondhand smoke are just as susceptible to the above occurrence, if not more so. Zinc deficiencies can lead to diminished senses of taste and smell, loss of appetite, and impaired wound healing. Long-term zinc deficiencies can result in lethargy, mental disturbances, skin changes, retarded growth, slow sexual maturation, hardening of the arteries, irregular menstrual cycles in teens, and sexual impotence in males.

CONCLUSION

I believe that trace minerals, especially in electrolyte form, are one of the most important and overlooked aspects of preventive and restorative health care of the twentieth century.

— Gillian Martlew, N.D., author of
"Electrolytes: The Spark of Life"

n the 1930s, vitamins were discovered, and everyone forgot about long-known minerals. We may be looking frantically for health in the wrong direction. We are made of minerals. Vitamins play their part, of course, but the minerals liberate the vitamins to do their work. Lacking vitamins, the system can make use of the minerals, but lacking minerals, the vitamins are useless, according to Charles Northern, M.D., one of the earliest nutritional physicians. Wayne Cook, a California mineral researcher, says: "Vitamins are found in greatest quantities where the greatest quantities of minerals occur. For it is impossible to find a plant that carries a full vitamin content unless minerals in large amounts are also present. Nature brings minerals into the leaf veins before she can begin to manufacture vitamins."

At no other time in history have the people of the world been so exposed to such a wide variety of pollutants in such high concentrations. If the body is healthy and functioning at its peak, it can generally detoxify and eliminate most of the pollutants without a great deal of damage. Three billion cells of the body die every minute. In good health or in youth when the mineral supply is high, these cells are replaced as fast as they die. But during aging or illness, when the mineral supply is depleted, the cell growth slows down and reproduction finally stops, resulting in death. Because prolonged mineral deficiencies cause many internal mechanisms to shut down, and minerals are so vital in initiating the actions of other substances to do their work, they must be given first consideration in acquiring or maintaining health.

Current research shows us that even when consuming the so-called "balanced diet," our food and water supply will not provide us with all the raw materials we need to maintain optimum health. Additionally, many of our prominent nutritional experts suggest, based on current data, that many of today's debilitating and chronic diseases, such as heart disease, strokes, hypertension, diabetes, and atherosclerosis, are caused by long-term nutritional deficiencies. Because of the body's inability to manufacture the mineral elements, maintaining proper mineral balances through supplementation is believed to be the most important part of the nutritional puzzle.

There is conclusive evidence that our farm and range soils are void of the necessary minerals we need. Studies have shown that our soils have 85-percent less of the same minerals they had 100 years ago. Recently, the World Health Organization reported that this figure is now 95-percent less. Based on current data and the unstable variability of minerals within our soils, which in turn causes severe mineral deficiencies in our food supply, it would be wise to consider the following options:

- Eat only fresh, whole grains and, if possible, only organically grown food.

- Eat five or six small meals a day instead of just one large meal to insure that proper utilization and digestion of food takes place.

- Supplement your diet with a multi-vitamin and -mineral formula.

- Use a liquid mineral formula that states that the minerals are in their electrolyte form daily.

- Stay away from bargain-basement nutritional formulas. Many of these types of supplements use inferior materials and transport agents that inhibit absorption of minerals.

- Consider the use of supplemental hydrochloric acid and other digestive aids, as they act as helpers to insure the proper use and absorption of mineral elements.

- Consider setting up a program with your health-care professional, assessing your current mineral electrolyte levels and what these levels should be in the future.

- Do not ignore the signs of possible mineral imbalances, such as dizziness, lightheadedness, cravings for sweets, dry skin, fatigue, depression, and brittle bones.

- Consult your health-care professional if you are experiencing any of these symptoms.

- Exercise regularly. This is very important for proper

calcium absorption and deposition in the bones to ensure good bone health and structure.

- Consume alcoholic beverages moderately. They act as diuretics and can cause unwanted loss of electrolytes.

- Become a mineral guru! Increase your knowledge about the life-giving aspects of these tiny powerhouses.

With all the overwhelming evidence of the effectiveness of the mineral electrolytes and their roles in preventive health care, further research is needed to validate the possible health-giving benefits of the other eighty-two elements known to exist thus far. With the astronomical cost to test, patent, and bring a drug to the market ($231 million on the average) compared with the preventive capabilities of mineral electrolytes, we may be looking unnecessarily in the wrong place for maintaining optimum health.

Today, scientists are doing more research in the area of the "electrolytic activity" of minerals, considered by many to be the forgotten keys to health. Dr. Bernard Jensen maintains that a new era of scientific investigation is emerging that will soon recognize and utilize the dominant force of these tiny powerhouses. This new era may be the most important to human development, amidst a society that practices treatment rather than the prevention of disease.

To insure that you are providing your system with the raw materials it needs on a day-to-day basis, new thinking about foods and the nutrients they provide and their value as medicine is emerging as a new science. Researchers maintain that the best way to meet daily nutrition needs is by including a liquid water-soluble, plant-derived mineral formula as part of a balanced diet.

GLOSSARY

adenosine triphosphate (ATP). A molecule present in all living cells that supplies energy to the cell for several biological processes.

antioxidants. Substances that act as nature's own protectors by controlling and minimizing free-radical reactions within the cell. Vitamin A, vitamin C, beta-carotene, vitamin E, selenium, and zinc are examples of antioxidants.

bioavailability. The degree to which a substance is available for absorption into the bloodstream.

chelation. The process of binding a substance to another to increase absorption.

colloidal dispersion. A suspension of finely divided particles that do not settle out of, and cannot be readily filtered from, the uniform medium in which they are dispersed.

crystalloid. A substance, like a crystal, that forms a true solution and can pass through a semipermeable membrane.

electrolyte. A substance whose molecules split into electrically charged particles, or ions, when melted or dissolved.

free radicals. An atom or group of atoms with at least one unpaired election, making it highly reactive with other atoms. Free radicals are produced during normal metabolism, but over time can cause a great deal of damage. They are produced in excess by external insults such as tobacco smoke, air pollution, ultraviolet light, and stress.

homeostasis. A state of balance or equilibrium in the body.

organic. A substance of, pertaining to, or derived from living organisms.

Appendix A.

COMPANIES THAT MAKE LIQUID MINERAL SUPPLEMENTS

While liquid mineral supplements are widely available, sometimes it is difficult to find them in conventional stores. The following companies produce liquid mineral supplements. You can contact these companies and order their products through the mail. Be aware that phone numbers and addresses are subject to change.

Albion Laboratories, Inc.
P.O. Box 750
101 North Main Street
Clearfield, UT 84015
(800) 453-2406 or
(801) 773-4631

Better Health Lab, Inc.
221 62nd Street
West New York, NJ 07093
(800) 810-1888

Future Biotics
72 Cotton Mill Hill
Brattleboro, VT 05301
(800) FOR-LIFE
(1-800-367-5433)

Naturopathic Research
   Labs, Inc.
P.O. Box 7594
North Port, FL 34287

The Rockland Corporation
12320 East Skelly Drive
Tulsa, OK 74128
(800) 258-5028

Trace Minerals Research
P.O. Box 429
Roy, UT 84067

Appendix B.

Companies That Test Blood Mineral Levels

The following companies will determine your blood mineral levels. Some companies require only a hair sample. Some companies require that your healh-care practitioner submit a blood sample. Contact a prospective company to find out what its general procedure is. Be aware that phone numbers and addresses are subject to change.

MetaMetrix Medical
  Laboratory
5000 Peachtree Industrial
  Blvd.
Suite 110
Norcross, GA 30071
(770) 446-5483 or
(800) 221-4640

Pantox Laboratories, Inc.
4622 Santa Fe Street
San Diego, CA 92109
(888) 726-8698

SpectraCell Laboratories,
  Inc.
515 Post Oak Boulevard
Suite 830
Houston, TX 77027
(713) 621-3101 or
(800) 227-5227

Trace Mineral Systems
115 S. Royal Street
Suite 141
Alexandria, VA 22314-3327
(703) 299-9306

REFERENCES

Chapter 1   Minerals: Nature's Biological Catalysts

Bosco, D. *The People's Guide to Vitamins and Minerals.* Chicago: Contemporary Books, 1994.

Cichoke, A.J. "Zinc: The Free Radical Fighter" *Let's Live* (January 1994): 32–36.

Clark, L. *Know Your Nutrition.* New Canaan, CT: Keats Publishing, 1973.

DiCyan, E. *Vitamins in Your Life and the Micronutrients.* New York: Simon and Schuster, 1974.

Garrison, R. and E. Somer. *The Nutritional Desk Reference.* New Canaan, CT: Keats Publishing, 1995.

Insel, P.M. and W.T. Roth. *Core Concepts in Health.* Mountainview, CA: Mayfield Publishing, 1988.

Maugh, T.H. "Longer Life Span in Rats Linked to Chromium." *Los Angeles Times* (Oct. 20, 1992).

Mindell, E. *Live Longer and Feel Better with Vitamins and Minerals.* New Canaan, CT: Keats Publishing, 1994.

Rogers, S.A. "How the Sick Get Sicker Without Nutritional Supplements." *Let's Live* 62 (2) (January 1994):44–47.

Schwartz, M. *Minerals, Self Care News*. San Antonio: Inner Health Group, Inc., 1996.

Wallach, J. *Dead Doctor's Don't Lie, Lecture Series on Mineral Research*. West Jordan, UT: Norton's Nutrition, 1995.

"Washington Update: President Enacts Food Quality Protection Act." *The Energy Times* (October 1996):18.

Williams, S.R. *Essentials of Nutrition and Diet Therapy*. St. Louis: C.V. Mosby Co., 1974.

Chapter 2   Minerals Are Electric

Buban, P. and M.L. Schmitt. *Understanding Electricity and Electronics*. 3d ed. New York: McGraw-Hill, 1975.

Cassata, C. "How to Balance Body Chemistry." *Let's Live* (March 1995):20–24.

Clark, L. *Know Your Nutrition*. New Canaan, CT: Keats Publishing, 1973.

Formulas for Health, A Comprehensive Guide to Enzymes, Health Guide No. 35. Green Bay, WI: Enzymatic Therapy, 1988.

Martlew, G. *Electrolytes: The Spark of Life*. Murdock, FL: Nature's Publishing Ltd., 1995.

Schroeder, H.A. *Trace Elements and Man*. Old Greenwich, CT: The Devine-Adair Company, 1975.

Schwartz, M. *Minerals Are Essential for Everybody*. San Antonio: Inner Health Group, Inc., 1995.

Wade, C. *Helping Your Health with Enzymes*. West Nyack, NY: Parker Publishing, 1966.

Weil, A. *Health and Healing*. New York: Houghton-Mifflin, 1995.

Chapter 3   The Antioxidant Connection

Cassata, C. "How to Balance Body Chemistry." *Let's Live* (March 1995):20–24.

Cichoke, A.J. "Zinc: The Free Radical Fighter." *Let's Live* (January 1994):32–36.

Cowley, Geoffrey, et. al. "The Vitamin Revolution." *Newsweek* (June 7, 1993):46–49.

Cutler, R.G. "Carotenoids and Retinol: Their Possible Importance in Determining Longevity of Primate Species." Proceedings of the National Academy of Sciences, 1984: 29–31.

Kronhausen, A., P. Kronhausen, and H.B. Dempoulous. *Formula For Life: The Antioxidant, Free Radical, Detoxification Program.* New York: William Morrow and Company, Inc., 1989.

Newslinks. "Symposium Explores Role of Antioxidants in Fighting Disease." *Whole Foods* (October 1995):4–5.

Passwater, R.A. *Selenium as Food and Medicine.* New Canaan, CT: Keats Publishing, 1980.

Pearson, D. and S. Shaw. *Life Extension: A Practical Scientific Approach.* New York: Warner Books, 1982.

Vleet Van, J.F. "Effect of Selenium-Vitamin E on Adriamycin-Induced Cardiomyopathy in Rabbits." *American Journal of Veterinary Research* 39 (1978):997–1010.

Weil, A. *Health and Healing.* New York: Houghton-Mifflin, 1995.

Willix, R.D. *You Can Feel Good All The Time.* Baltimore: Health for Life, 1994.

Chapter 4 The Absorption Problem

Ahlson, C.B. *Health From the Sea and Soil.* Jericho, NY: Exposition Press, 1962.

All Vitamins Are Not Created Equal. Long Beach, CA: Nature's Plus, 1990.

Bland, J. *Assess Your Own Nutritional Status.* New Canaan, CT: Keats Publishing, 1987.

Callewaert, D.E. and J. Genyea. *Basic Chemistry.* New York: Worth Publishers, 1980.

Clark, L. *Know Your Nutrition.* New Canaan, CT: Keats Publishing, 1973.

Colloidal Confusion, or A Rose By Any Other Name. North Point, FL: Naturopathic Research, 1994.

Dunne, L.T. *Nutrition Almanac.* 3d ed. New York: McGraw-Hill, 1990.

Formulas for Health, A Comprehensive Guide to Enzymes, Health Guide No. 35.: Green Bay, WI: Enzymatic Therapy, 1988.

Fox, A. and B. Fox. "An Exciting New Frontier in Nutritional Testing." *Let's Live* (October 1994):38.

Future Biotics. "Advanced Colloidal Minerals." *Health Food Business* (January 1995):17.

Guyton, A.C. *Function of the Human Body.* Philadelphia: W.B. Sanders Co., 1969.

Kervan, L. *Biological Transmutations.* Binghamton, NY: Swan House Publishing, 1972.

Parker, Sybil P. *McGraw-Hill Enclyopedia of Science and Technology.* 5th ed. New York: McGraw-Hill Publications, 1982.

Nerbrand, C., K. Svardsudd, and G. Tibblin. "Cardiovascular Mortality and Morbidity in Seven Counties in Sweden in Relation to Water Hardness and Geological Settings." *European Heart Journal* 13 (1992):721–727.

Stanway, A. *Biochemic Tissue Salts, A Natural Way to Prevent and Cure Illness.* Wellingborough, Northamptonshire, England: Thorsons Publishing Group, 1987.

Starr, C. and R. Taggart. *Biology: The Unity and Diversity of Life.* Belmont, CA: Wadsworth Publishing, 1987.

Stockton, S. "Muddy Water." *Sarasota Report* Vol. 5, No. 5 (June 1995).

Is the Truth About Your Trace Minerals Crystal Clear or Clear as Mud?. Roy, UT: Trace Mineral Research, 1996.

Ward, J.A. and H.R. Hertzel. *Biology Today and Tomorrow*. St. Paul, MN: West Publishing, 1987.

Williams, J. *The Wonderful World Within You*. New York: Bantam Books, 1977.

Part Two   The Minerals

Airola, P. *How to Get Well*. Phoenix: Health Plus Publishers, 1987.

Alfin-Slater, R.B. and D. Kritchevsky. *Human Nutrition: A Complete Treatise—The Adult Macronutrients*. New York: Plenum Press, 1980.

Clark, L. *Know Your Nutrition*. New Canaan, CT: Keats Publishing, 1973.

Crain, L. *Magic Vitamins and Organic Foods*. Los Angeles: Crandrich Studios, 1976.

Davis, A. *Let's Stay Healthy: A Guide to Lifelong Nutrition*. New York: Harcourt Brace Jovanovich, Inc., 1981.

DiCyan, E. *Vitamins in Your Life and the Micronutrients*. New York: Simon and Schuster, 1974.

Dunne, L.T. *Nutrition Almanac*. 3d ed. New York: McGraw-Hill, 1990.

Forecast of the U.S. Mineral Supplements Market. New York: Packaged Facts, 1991.

Garrison, R. and E. Somer. *The Nutritional Desk Reference*. New Canaan, CT: Keats Publishing, 1995.

Guthrie, H.A. *Introductory Nutrition*. 2d ed. St. Louis: C. V. Mosby, 1971.

Hendler, S.S. *The Complete Guide to Anti-Aging Nutrients*. New York: Simon and Schuster, 1985.

Hoffer, A. and M. Walker. *Ortho-Molecular Nutrition.* New Canaan, CT: Keats Publishing, 1978.

Insel, P.M. and W.T. Roth. *Core Concepts in Health.* Mountainview, CA: Mayfield Publishing, 1988.

Kirschmann, J.D. *Nutritional Almanac.* New York: McGraw-Hill, 1975.

Latour, J.P. *The ABCs of Vitamins and Minerals.* New York: Arco Publishing, 1978.

Martlew, G. *Electrolytes: The Spark of Life.* Murdock, FL: Nature's Publishing Ltd., 1995.

McNutt, K.W. and D.R. McNutt. *Nutrition and Food Choices.* Chicago: Science Research Associates, 1978.

Mindell, E. *The Vitamin Bible.* New York: Warner Books, 1985.

_____. *What You Should Know About Trace Minerals.* New Canaan, CT: Keats Publishing, 1997.

National Research Council. *Recommended Dietary Allowances.* 8th ed. Washington, DC: National Academy of Sciences, 1974.

National Research Council. *Recommended Dietary Allowances.* 10th ed. Washington, DC: National Academy of Sciences, 1989.

Pearson, D. and S. Shaw. *Life Extension: A Practical Scientific Approach.* New York: Warner Books, 1982.

Prevention Magazine and Health Books. *The Doctor's Book of Home Remedies.* Emmaus, PA: Rodale Press, 1990.

_____. *Complete Book of Minerals for Health.* PA: Rodale Press, 1981.

Quillin, P. *Healing Nutrients.* Chicago: Contempory Books, 1987.

Ruben, D. *Everything You Always Wanted to Know About Nutrition.* New York: Avon Publishing, 1978.

Schauss, A.G. *Minerals and Human Health, The Rationale for Optimal and Balanced Trace Element Levels.* Tacoma, WA: Life Science Press, 1995.

Schroeder, H.A. *Trace Elements and Man*. Old Greenwich, CT: The Devine-Adair Company, 1975.

Shils, M.E. and V.R. Young. *Modern Nutrition in Health and Disease*. 7th ed. Philadelphia: Lea and Febiger, 1988.

Underwood, E.J. *Trace Elements in Human and Animal Nutrition*. 3d ed. New York: Academic Press, 1971.

Vaughn, L. *The Complete Book of Vitamins and Minerals For Health*. Emmaus, PA: Rodale Press, 1988.

Williams, S.R. *Essentials of Nutrition and Diet Therapy*. St. Louis: The C. V. Mosby Company, 1974.

Chapter 5   Calcium

Caddell, J.L. "Magnesium Deficiency in Protein-Calorie Malnutrition: A Follow-Up Study." *Annals of the New York Academy of Sciences* 162 (1969): 874.

Heinrich, E.G. *The Power of a Complete Spectrum of Minerals*. Tulsa: The Rockland Corporation, 1996.

Kozlovshy, K., et al. "Effects of Diets High in Simple Sugars on Urinary Calcium Losses." *Metabolism* 35 (6) (1986): 515–518.

Licata, A. and D. Jones-Gall. "Effect of Supplemental Calcium on Serum and Urinary Calcium in Osteoporosis Patients." *Journal of the American College of Nutrition* 11 (March 1992): 164–167.

National Research Council. *Diet and Health Implications for Reducing Chronic Disease Risk*. Washington, DC: National Academy Press, 1989.

Reed, P.B. *Nutrition: An Applied Science*. St. Paul, MN: West Publishing Co., 1980.

Chapter 6   Chloride

Fredricks, Carlton. *Nutrition Guide For The Prevention and Cure of Common Ailments and Diseases*. New York: Simon and Schuster, 1982.

Fredericks, Carlton and H. Bailey. *Food Facts and Fallacies.* New York: Arco Publishing Co., 1976.

National Research Council. *Toxicants Occurring Naturally in Foods.* Washington, DC: National Academy of Sciences, 1973.

Starr, C. and R. Taggart. *Biology: The Unity and Diversity of Life.* Belmont, CA: Wadsworth Publishing, 1987.

Vaughn, L. *The Complete Book of Vitamins and Minerals For Health.* Emmaus, PA: Rodale Press, 1988.

Chapter 7   Magnesium

Aikawa, J.K. *The Role of Magnesium in Biologic Processes.* Springfield, IL: Charles. C. Thomas, 1963.

Colgan, M. *Your Personal Vitamin Profile.* New York: William Morrow and Company, 1982.

Martin, H.E., J. Mehl, and M. Wertman. "Clinical Studies of Magnesium Metabolism." *Medical Clinics of North America* 36 (1952):1157.

National Research Council. *Toxicants Occurring Naturally in Foods.* Washington, DC: National Academy of Sciences, 1973.

Paolisso, G., S. Sgambato, and A. Gambardella. "Daily Magnesium Supplements Improve Glucose Handling in Elderly Subjects." *American Journal of Clinical Nutrition* 55 (1992): 1161–1167.

Pike, R.L. and M.L. Brown. *Nutrition: An Integrated Approach.* New York: John Wiley and Sons, 1984.

Rogers, S.A. "How the Sick Get Sicker Without Nutritional Supplements." *Let's Live* 62 (1) (January 1994):44–47.

Seelig, M. "Interrelationship of Magnesium and Estrogen in Cardiovascular and Bone Disorders, Eclampsia, Migraine and Premenstrual Syndrome." *Journal of the American College of Nutrition* 12 (1993): 422–458.

Shils, M.E. "Magnesium." In *Modern Nutrition in Health and Disease,* 5th ed, ed. R.S. Goodhart and M.E. Shils, pp. 287–296. Philadelphia: Lea and Febiger, 1975.

Trimmer, E. *The Magic of Magnesium.* Rochester, VT: Thorsons Publishing Group, 1987.

Wacker, W.E.C. and A.F. Parisi. "Magnesium Metabolism." *New England Journal of Medicine* 278 (1968): 712.

Chapter 8 Phosphorus

Pike, R.L. and M.L. Brown. *Nutrition: An Integrated Approach.* New York: John Wiley and Sons, 1984.

Starr, C. and R. Taggart. *Biology: The Unity and Diversity of Life.* Belmont, CA: Wadsworth Publishing, 1987.

Van Sydow, G. "A Study of the Development of Melcots in Premature Infants." *ActaPaediatrica Scandinavia* Suppl. 33 (2)(1946).

Chapter 9 Potassium

Addison, W.L.T. "The Uses of Sodium Chloride, Potassium Chloride, Sodium Bromide, and Potassium Bromide in Cases of Arterial Hypertension Which Are Amenable to Potassium Chloride." *Canadian Medical Association Journal* 18 (April 1928): 281.

He, J., et al. "Effect of Dietary Electrolytes Upon Calcium Excretion: The Yi People Study." *Journal of Hypertension* 10 (1992): 671–676.

Wilde, W.S. "Potassium." In: *Mineral Metabolism,* Vol. 2, Part B, ed. C. L. Comar and F. Bronner, pp. 73–107. New York: Academic Press, 1962.

Chapter 10 Sodium

Dahl, L.K. "Salt and Hypertension." *New England Journal of Medicine* 25 (1972): 231.

_____. "Salt Intake and Salt Need." *New England Journal of Medicine* 258 (1958): 1152, 1205.

National Research Council. *Toxicants Occuring Naturally in Foods.* Washington, DC: National Academy of Sciences, 1973.

Pike, R.L. and H.A. Smicliklas. "A Reappraisal of Sodium Restriction During Pregnancy." *International Journal of Gynecology and Obstetrics* 10 (1972): 1.

Chapter 11   Sulfur

Passwater, R.A. *Selenium as Food and Medicine.* New Canaan, CT: Keats Publishing, 1980.

Chapter 12   Chromium

Anderson, R.A., et al. "Exercise Effect on Chromium Excretion of Trained and Untrained Men Consuming a Constant Diet." *Journal of Applied Physiology* 64 (1988): 249.

Anderson, R.A. and A.S. Kozlovsky. "Chromium Intake, Absorption, and Excretion of Subjects Consuming Self-Selected Diets." *American Journal of Clinical Nutrition* 41 (1985): 1177–1183.

Brody, J. *Jane Brody's Nutrition Book.* New York: W. W. Norton, 1981.

Evans, G. "The Effect of Chromium Picolinate on Insulin Controlled Parameters in Humans." *International Journal of Biosocial and Medical Research* 11 (2) (1989):163–180.

Fisher, J.A. *The Chromium Program.* New York: Harper and Row, 1990.

Gormely, J.J. "Liquid Nutrition." *Better Nutrition For Today's Living* (April 13, 1996): 36.

Levander, O.A. "Selenium and Chromium in Human Nutrition." *Journal of American Dietary Association* 66 (1975): 338.

Mayer, J. *Human Nutrition.* Springfield, IL: Charles C. Thomas, 1964.

Mertz, W. "Chromium Occurrence and Function in Biological Systems." *Physiological Review* 49 (1969):163.

Mossop, R.T. "Glucose Tolerance in Adult Diabetes." *Central African Journal of Medicine* 29 (1983): 80.

Passwater, R.A. *GTF Chromium.* New Canaan, CT: Keats Publishing, 1982.

Salaman, M. *Foods That Heal.* Menlo Park, CA: James Stafford Publishing, 1996.

Schauss, A.G. *Minerals and Human Health: The Rationale for Optimal and Balanced Trace Element Levels.* Tacoma, WA: Life Science Press, 1995.

Schroeder, H.A. "The Role of Chromium in Mamalian Nutrition." *American Journal of Clinical Nutrition* 21(1968): 230–244.

Schwartz, K. and W. Mertz. "Glucose Tolerance Factors and Its Differentiation From Factor 3." *Archives of Biochemistry and Biophysics* 72 (1957): 515.

Simonoff, M. "Chromium Deficiency and Cardiovascular Risk." *Cardiovascular Research* 18 (1984): 591–596.

Stanway, A. *Biochemic Tissue Salts: A Natural Way to Prevent and Cure Illness.* Thorsons Publishing Group, Wellingborough, Northamptonshire, England, 1987.

Chapter 13   Cobalt

Beck, W.S. "Deoxyribonucleotide Synthesis and the Role of Vitamin B_{12} in Erythropoiesis." *Vitamins and Hormones* 26 (1968): 413.

Brody, J. *Jane Brody's Nutrition Book.* New York: W. W. Norton, 1981.

Castle, W.B. and G.R. Minot. *Pathological Physiology and Clinical Description of Anemias.* New York: Oxford University Press, 1936.

FAO/WHO (Food and Agriculture Organization/World Health Organization). "Requirements of Absorbic Acid, Vitamin D, Vitamin B_{12}, Folate and Iron." *World Health Organization Technical Report Services* 452 (1970).

Gormely, J.J. "Liquid Nutrition." *Better Nutrition For Today's Living* (April 13, 1996): 36.

Salaman, M. *Foods That Heal.* Menlo Park, CA: James Stafford Publishing, 1996.

Schauss, A.G. *Minerals and Human Health: The Rationale for Optimal and Balanced Trace Element Levels.* Tacoma, WA: Life Science Press, 1995.

Stanway, A. *Biochemic Tissue Salts: A Natural Way to Prevent and Cure Illness.* Thorsons Publishing Group, Wellingborough, Northamptonshire, England, 1987.

Chapter 14   Copper

Brody, J. *Jane Brody's Nutrition Book.* New York: W. W. Norton, 1981.

Carnes, W.H. "Role of Copper in Corrective Tissue Metabolism." *Federation Proceeding, Federation of the American Society for Experimental Biology* 30 (1971): 955.

Cartwright, C.E. and M.M. Wintrobe. "Copper Metabolism in Normal Subjects." *American Journal of Clinical Nutrition* 14 (1964): 224.

Chaney, M.S. and M.L. Rose. *Nutrition.* 8th ed. Boston: Houghton-Mifflin Co., 1971.

Finnegan, M. "Freedom Movement." *The Energy Times* (March/April 1995): 50–54.

Gormely, J.J. "Liquid Nutrition." *Better Nutrition For Today's Living* (April 13, 1996): 36.

Hunsaker, H.A., M. Morita, and K.G.D. Allen. "Marginal Copper Deficiency in Rats." *Atherosclerosis* 51 (1984): 1–19.

Salaman, M. *Foods That Heal.* Menlo Park, CA: James Stafford Publishing, 1996.

Schauss, A.G. *Minerals and Human Health: The Rationale for Optimal and Balanced Trace Element Levels.* Tacoma, WA: Life Science Press, 1995.

Stanway, A. *Biochemic Tissue Salts: A Natural Way to Prevent and Cure Illness.* Thorsons Publishing Group, Wellingborough, Northamptonshire, England, 1987.

Chapter 15   Fluorine

Brody, J. *Jane Brody's Nutrition Book.* New York: W. W. Norton, 1981.

Gormely, J.J. "Liquid Nutrition." *Better Nutrition For Today's Living* (April 13, 1996): 36.

Pak, C., K. Sakhace, and V. Piziak. "Slow-Release Sodium Fluoride in the Management of Post Menopausal Osteoporosis." *Annals of Internal Medicine* 120 (1994): 625–632.

Salaman, M. *Foods That Heal.* Menlo Park, CA: James Stafford Publishing, 1996.

Schauss, A.G. *Minerals and Human Health: The Rationale for Optimal and Balanced Trace Element Levels.* Tacoma, WA: Life Science Press, 1995.

Stanway, A. *Biochemic Tissue Salts: A Natural Way to Prevent and Cure Illness.* Thorsons Publishing Group, Wellingborough, Northamptonshire, England, 1987.

Chapter 16   Iodine

Brody, J. *Jane Brody's Nutrition Book.* New York: W. W. Norton, 1981.

Gormely, J.J. "Liquid Nutrition." *Better Nutrition For Today's Living* (April 13, 1996): 36.

Guyton, A.C. *Function of the Human Body.* Philadelphia: W.B. Sanders Co., 1969.

Pittman, J.A. *Diagnosis and Treatment of Thyroid Diseases.* Philadelphia: F.A. Davis Company, 1963.

Salaman, M. *Foods That Heal.* Menlo Park, CA: James Stafford Publishing, 1996.

Schauss, A.G. *Minerals and Human Health: The Rationale for Optimal and Balanced Trace Element Levels.* Tacoma, WA: Life Science Press, 1995.

Stanway, A. *Biochemic Tissue Salts: A Natural Way to Prevent and Cure Illness.* Thorsons Publishing Group, Wellingborough, Northamptonshire, England, 1987.

Chapter 17   Iron

Brody, J. *Jane Brody's Nutrition Book*. New York: W. W. Norton, 1981.

Castle, W.B. and G.R. Minot. *Pathological Physiology and Clinical Description of Anemias*. New York: Oxford University Press, 1936.

Gormely, J.J. "Liquid Nutrition." *Better Nutrition For Today's Living* (April 13, 1996): 36.

Herbert, N. "Megaloblastic Anemia." In *Textbook of Medicine*, 14th ed, ed. P. B. Beeson and W. McDermott, pp. 1404–1413. Philadelphia: W. B. Sanders, 1975.

Macara, I.G., T.G. Hoy, and P.M. Harrison. "Formation of Ferritin From Apoferritin, Kinetics and Mechanism of Iron Uptake." *Biochemistry Journal* 126 (1972): 151.

Mayer, J. *Human Nutrition*. Springfield, IL: Charles C. Thomas, 1964.

McCollum, E. *A History of Nutrition*. Boston: Houghton-Mifflin, 1957.

Salaman, M. *Foods That Heal*. Menlo Park, CA: James Stafford Publishing, 1996.

Schauss, A.G. *Minerals and Human Health: The Rationale for Optimal and Balanced Trace Element Levels*. Tacoma, WA: Life Science Press, 1995.

Stanway, A. *Biochemic Tissue Salts: A Natural Way to Prevent and Cure Illness*. Thorsons Publishing Group, Wellingborough, Northamptonshire, England, 1987.

Chapter 18   Manganese

Brody, J. *Jane Brody's Nutrition Book*. New York: W. W. Norton, 1981.

Hauser, R.A., et al. "Blood Manganese Correlates with Brain Magnetic Resonance Imaging Changes in Patients with Liver Disease." *Canadian Journal of Neurological Sciences* 23(2)(1996): 95–98.

Megafood. *Megafood Grown from Nutrients.* Derry, NH: Bioson Laboratories, Inc., 1995.

O'ambrosia, E., et al. "Glucosamine Sulfate: A Controlled Clinical Investigation in Arthritis." *Pharmatherapeutica* 2 (1991): 504–508.

Salaman, M. *Foods That Heal.* Menlo Park, CA: James Stafford Publishing, 1996.

Schauss, A.G. *Minerals and Human Health: The Rationale for Optimal and Balanced Trace Element Levels.* Tacoma, WA: Life Science Press, 1995.

Stanway, A. *Biochemic Tissue Salts: A Natural Way to Prevent and Cure Illness.* Thorsons Publishing Group, Wellingborough, Northamptonshire, England, 1987.

Chapter 19 Molybdenum

Brody, J. *Jane Brody's Nutrition Book.* New York: W. W. Norton, 1981.

Gormely, J.J. "Liquid Nutrition." *Better Nutrition For Today's Living* (April 13, 1996): 36.

Schauss, A.G. *Minerals and Human Health: The Rationale for Optimal and Balanced Trace Element Levels.* Tacoma, WA: Life Science Press, 1995.

Stanway, A. *Biochemic Tissue Salts: A Natural Way to Prevent and Cure Illness.* Thorsons Publishing Group, Wellingborough, Northamptonshire, England, 1987.

Chapter 20 Selenium

Brody, J. *Jane Brody's Nutrition Book.* New York: W. W. Norton, 1981.

Gormely, J.J. "Liquid Nutrition." *Better Nutrition For Today's Living* (April 13, 1996): 36.

Hausman, P. *Foods that Fight Cancer.* New York: Rawson Associates, 1983.

Mindell, E. *Live Longer and Feel Better with Vitamins and Minerals.* New Canaan, CT: Keats Publishing, 1994.

Proceedings of the Symposium on Selenium-Telurium in the Environment held May 13, 1976 at the University of Notre Dame. Pittsburgh: Industrial Health Foundation, 1976, p. 253.

Salaman, M. *Foods That Heal.* Menlo Park, CA: James Stafford Publishing, 1996.

Schauss, A.G. *Minerals and Human Health: The Rationale for Optimal and Balanced Trace Element Levels.* Tacoma, WA: Life Science Press, 1995.

Schoene, N.W., V.C. Morris, and O.A. Levander. "Altered Arachidonic Acid Metabolism in Platelets and Aortas From Selenium-Deficient Rats." *Nutrition Research* 6 (1986): 75–83.

Schrauzer, G.N., et al. "Soil Levels of Selenium and Related Cancer Incidence." *Bioinorganic Chemistry* 7 (1977): 23.

Scott, M.L. "The Selenium Dilemma." *Journal of Nutrition* 103 (1971):803.

Shapiro, J.R. "Selenium and Carcinogenesis: A Review." *Annals of the New York Academy of Sciences* (1972): 192–215.

Stanway, A. *Biochemic Tissue Salts: A Natural Way to Prevent and Cure Illness.* Thorsons Publishing Group, Wellingborough, Northamptonshire, England, 1987.

Chapter 21 Zinc

Brody, J. *Jane Brody's Nutrition Book.* New York: W. W. Norton, 1981.

Gipoulox, J.D. "Zinc Levels and Cell Division." *Roux's Archives of Developmental Biology* 195 (1986): 193.

Gormely, J.J. "Liquid Nutrition." *Better Nutrition For Today's Living* (April 13, 1996): 36.

Hennig, B. and M. A. Stuart. "Nutrients That May Protect Against Artherosclerotic Lesion Formation." *Journal of Applied Nutrition,* 40 (1) (Spring 1988): 13–21.

Hennig, B., Y. Wang, and S. Ramasamy. "Zinc Deficiency Alters Barrier Function of Cultured Porcine Endothelial Cells." *Journal of Nutrition* 122 (1992): 1242–1247.

Salaman, M. *Foods That Heal.* Menlo Park, CA: James Stafford Publishing, 1996.

Schauss, A.G. *Minerals and Human Health: The Rationale for Optimal and Balanced Trace Element Levels.* Tacoma, WA: Life Science Press, 1995.

Stanway, A. *Biochemic Tissue Salts: A Natural Way to Prevent and Cure Illness.* Thorsons Publishing Group, Wellingborough, Northamptonshire, England, 1987.

Conclusion

Bland J. *Medical Applications of Clinical Nutrition.* New Canaan, CT: Keats Publishing, 1983.

Clark, L. *Know Your Nutrition.* New Canaan, CT: Keats Publishing, 1973.

Drake, D. and Uhlman, M. *Making Medicine Making Money.* Kansas City, MO: Andrews and McMeel Publishers, 1993.

Martlew, G. *Electrolytes: The Spark of Life.* Murdock, FL: Nature's Publishing Ltd., 1995.

Mindell, E. *Live Longer and Feel Better with Vitamins and Minerals.* New Canaan, CT: Keats Publishing, 1994.

Suggested Readings

Berger, Stuart. *Dr. Berger's Immune Power Diet*. New York: New American Library, 1985.

Borsook, H. *Vitamins*. New York: Pyramid Books, 1971.

Crain, L. *Magic Vitamins and Organic Foods*. Los Angeles: Crandrich Studios, 1976.

DiCyan, E. *A Beginner's Introduction to Trace Minerals*. New Canaan, CT: Keats Publishing, 1984.

Fisher, J.A. *The Chromium Program*. New York: Harper and Row, 1990.

Fredricks, Carlton. *Nutrition Guide for the Prevention and Cure of Common Ailments and Diseases*. New York: Simon and Schuster, 1982.

L'Abbé, B., Forbidden Secrets, Lecture Series with Dr. Chuck Conniry, Ph.D., Life Talk, 1996.

Latour, J.P. *The ABCs of Vitamins and Minerals*. New York: Arco Publishing, 1978.

Mathews, A.P. *Physiological Chemistry*. 5th ed. New York: William Wood and Company, 1930.

National Research Council. *Recommended Dietary Allowances.* 10th Revised Edition. Washington, D.C.: National Academy of Sciences, 1989.

Passwater, Richard A. *GTF Chromium.* New Canaan, CT: Keats Publishing, Inc., 1982.

Thomas, Lewis. *The Lives of a Cell.* New York: Bantam Books, 1980.

Wallach, J. *Dead Doctors Don't Lie, Lecture Series on Mineral Research.* West Jordan, UT: Norton's Nutrition, 1995.

INDEX

177